CREEPY-MOUSE
Coming To Get You

Barbara Holland

Clarion Books
TICKNOR & FIELDS : A HOUGHTON MIFFLIN COMPANY
New York

Clarion Books
Ticknor & Fields, a Houghton Mifflin Company
Copyright © 1985 by Barbara Holland

Library of Congress Cataloging in Publication Data
Holland, Barbara.
　Creepy-Mouse coming to get you.

　Summary: A young boy finds that it is up to him
to shield his sister and baby nephew from her quick-
tempered husband, recently released from prison.
　1. Children's stories, American. [1. Family
problems — Fiction] I. Title.
PZ7.H70815Cr　1985　　[Fic]　　84-14202
ISBN 0-89919-329-3

s　10　9　8　7　6　5　4　3　2　1

CREEPY-MOUSE
Coming To Get You

One

THE PHONE RANG, and Jeremy answered it because he was closer. He heard coins dropping. Somebody was calling from a pay phone, and a pay phone a long way off because the coins kept clanging down over and over before a man's voice said, "Is Rosalie there?"

"Just a minute. It's for you," Jeremy said, and his sister padded across the kitchen with her baby in its backpack peering over her shoulder.

"Hello?" she said. "*Mack?* Where are you? You're out?"

Out. Jeremy wondered if it was polite to say that, when a person got out of jail. Maybe you should pretend they'd just been sick, or away on vacation. He didn't know. Rosalie wouldn't know either. They weren't exactly the kind of people who had a lot of friends in jail all the time.

Mack was Rosalie's husband, and he'd been in jail in Sheridan, Wyoming, but it wasn't as exciting as it sounded. Nothing Western like train robbery or cattle rustling. Just three months for getting drunk and wrecking his truck and trying to punch a state trooper. He hadn't even hit the trooper, Rosalie said. Just swung at him and missed and fell down. After that their mother sent her the plane fare to come home with the baby. Jeremy and his mother had never even seen Mack, just a picture of a man in a checked shirt squinting into the sun.

On the phone Rosalie was saying, "But I didn't really run off and leave you. I mean, I did, but what else could I do? Just sit in the trailer with your mother and stepfather and wait? And there wasn't any money."

She was backing up, trying to get away from the phone on the wall. The baby on her back bumped into the refrigerator.

"No, I can't come out there. On a bus? But that takes so long, and with the baby and all, and I don't have any money. What? Come and get me? Mack — wait —"

Jeremy heard the operator's voice saying, "If you wish an additional three minutes, please deposit two dollars and sixty-five cents," and then the click.

Rosalie stared at the phone. The baby reached for it across her shoulder. After a while it made a nasty buzzing noise and Rosalie hung it up.

"He's coming here," she said.

"Where will he sleep?" asked Jeremy, and then his face got hot. Naturally Mack would sleep with Rosalie; she was married to him. That was hard to remember if you'd never seen her with a husband. She didn't look very married, with her short, thick yellow braids, and she still carried around that same little black notebook, to write her poems in. She always had the baby in its backpack or slung down her front in a kind of cloth pocket, but it didn't make her look married. She looked like a sister baby-sitting, and the baby might have been Jeremy himself ten years ago.

She whispered something to herself, staring at the phone.

"What?" said Jeremy.

"He's mad. Mack. He says I shouldn't have run off. He's not coming here to stay, he's coming to take me and the baby."

"Back to Wyoming?" Jeremy loved the sound of the word *Wyoming*. When Rosalie had gone out there to college he used to tell everyone where she was, just to say the word. It sounded big. It was nice to have her home again, but maybe, if she went back, he could go and visit her. See the mountains.

"No," she said. "Texas. He thinks he can get work there." She looked scared.

"Oh." Jeremy spilled some salt on the table and drew pictures in it. This wasn't his department. His mother should be here, but she was working double shifts at her hostess job now, till she paid off Rosalie's plane fare, and she was hardly ever home. "Maybe that would be nice. Texas. You could get a horse."

"You don't *understand*," she cried. "I said, he's *mad*. He said people don't treat Mack like that, and he's going to punish me."

"Do you think he'd hit you?"

Her eyes went shiny with tears and she ran out of the kitchen with the baby lurching around in his pack and grabbing for one of her braids. Her feet thumped upstairs to her room.

Jeremy swept the salt off onto the floor. It was none of his business. She shouldn't have married this Mack if she didn't like him. He sat for a while at the kitchen table and then noticed that his watch had stopped running. In fact, it said 12:17, so it must have stopped hours ago. He wound it and listened, but nothing happened. He shook it and then banged it on the table. Nothing. He decided to take it apart, and rummaged in all the drawers and then found a nail file on the windowsill. He pried the back off and looked inside. It was full of little wheels fastened down with tiny screws.

Kelly banged on the kitchen door and signaled him to come out. He waved at her to come in, and she pushed open the door. "Aren't you coming to work on the hut?"

"The fort? Yeah, I guess so." Kelly always called it a hut, but that sounded like a place where poor people lived in King Arthur times, and kept a pig. A fort sounded more like armies on horseback, but Kelly couldn't see the difference. Kelly was stubborn. "I want to do this first," he said.

With the tip of the nail file he unscrewed the little gears or whatever and poked them out of the watch onto a napkin.

"You're fixing your watch?"

"Don't be silly," he said. Kelly was as bad as Mom, the way they thought he was good with machinery and fixing things, when actually he didn't know anything about them. They just thought that because he was a boy. "Nobody can fix a watch," he said. "I'm just taking it apart."

She watched over his shoulder. "What's that for? That thing that bounces back and forth?"

"How should I know?" Suddenly he was sick of the watch and wadded up the napkin with all the tiny stuff in it and threw it in the trash. "Rosalie's husband's coming to get her."

"I thought he was in jail."

"He got out."

"You mean escaped?"

"No, I don't think so. His time was finished."

Kelly lost interest. "Let's go work on the hut."

"The fort."

It was a good fort, much solider than the ones he used to build when he was little. They always had about a million nails in every board, but they fell down anyway. This one stood square and didn't lean over because Kelly leveled everything with a spirit level she'd gotten for her birthday. That was Kelly's business, building things. When she grew up she was going to be a builder. She had it all planned. If she could get in, and there was money enough, she was going to the kind of college where you get an engineering degree and build bridges and tunnels. Otherwise, she would be a plain builder of houses. The fort was practice for her, and everything had to be just right.

Jeremy thought it would be nice to have your whole life planned like that. His own life in front of him didn't look like much. He'd get some kind of job, he supposed, and just go to the office and come back. Maybe be a sales manager like his father in Baltimore, and sit at a desk making phone calls while Kelly was out building bridges.

The fort was in a patch of woods at Maple Road and Spring Street, where nobody had gotten around to building anything yet. Nobody but Jeremy and Kelly.

"That corner shows," said Kelly. "We have to put some more stuff over it. You can see it from Spring Street."

"More of those pricker bushes?" said Jeremy. "I'm still bleeding from last time. What difference does it make anyway? Nobody cares what we do in the woods here, at least not till they need it for something."

"Somebody'd care. They'd make us tear it down."

"Why?"

"Oh, I don't know." Kelly picked up a stone and threw it at a tree and missed. "Because it might fall on our heads. Because some little kid might come along and get trapped in it. When grownups want to say no, they can always think of a million weird reasons. We might play with matches and set fire to it. We might be looking at each other with no clothes on."

"Don't be gross."

"*I'm* not gross. Grownups are. They think about stuff like that all the time. Where's the shovel?"

"Inside." Jeremy wormed his way through the bush they'd left growing in front of the secret entrance and went in on his hands and knees. Inside, you could stand up straight at the high side, and the roof was waterproof unless it rained really hard.

The shovel was in the corner, under the blue jacket he kept forgetting to take home. Its handle was broken off short, but they used it, stamping on it and scraping away, to dig up vines and pricker bushes. That was another one of Kelly's rules. They had to use live, planted things to hide the walls, because if they just piled up cut stuff it would turn brown, and look different from the rest of the woods.

When Jeremy picked up the shovel there was a snake behind it.

He gave a yelp, and then he was embarrassed. He didn't mind snakes, really. He kind of liked them as long as he knew they were there. It was unexpected snakes that surprised him.

Kelly poked her head through the doorway. "What happened?"

"A snake." It uncoiled slowly and started across the dirt floor like something pouring out of a bottle. It was big, longer than Jeremy's arm, but it was only a garter snake, with a garter snake's three yellow stripes running clear along it.

"Get it!" cried Kelly.

Jeremy dived for the snake and grabbed it with both hands. It thrashed strongly and hissed at him, showing the pale inside of its mouth.

"Don't let it bite you," said Kelly.

"They're not poisonous."

"They bite anyway."

The snake felt cool in his hands, and smooth but ridgy, like a waxed rope. It was amazingly strong. Jeremy crawled through the doorway on his elbows and came out into the daylight.

Kelly stroked the snake with her finger. "Let's keep

it. There's a fish tank in our basement that we can't keep fish in because it leaks, but it's got a lid."

"We can call it Glatisant," said Jeremy.

"That's a stupid name."

"It's not, it's in King Arthur. It was a kind of a dragon that barked like a whole lot of dogs."

"Great, a barking snake. You and your dumb King Arthur. Nobody reads books like that anymore. Come on, let's take it to my house. If we go in the back and straight down to the basement, Mom won't see us."

On the sidewalk they passed a little kid on a Big Wheel and Jeremy showed him Glatisant. The kid screamed and scrambled off the Big Wheel and ran for home, calling "Mommy!"

In Kelly's dark, moldy-smelling basement they found the fish tank and wiped the dust out and put the snake in. It poured itself around and around the glass walls, flickering its tongue at them and trying to understand why it couldn't get out.

They got some leaves and sticks from the garden to make it a bed, and some scraps of raw hamburger from the refrigerator. After a while Glatisant stopped struggling and lay still in the leaves and stared at nothing.

"I ought to get back home," said Jeremy.

"What for? It isn't six yet."

"I ought to go see about Rosalie, I guess. She was crying."

"Why? Her husband's coming, isn't he? She must be glad."

"She isn't. He wants to take her and the baby away. To Texas, she said."

"Well, he's her husband. If you're married and your husband wants to go somewhere, you have to go with him." Kelly poked Glatisant and made him squirm. "That's why I'm never going to get married."

"I think she's kind of scared of him," Jeremy said.

"That's dumb. Why would she marry somebody she was scared of?"

"I don't know. She's always doing something weird."

"Anyway, it's got nothing to do with you, does it?" Kelly was studying the basement floor. She scuffed a shoe across it and said, "Listen, I was thinking the hut ought to have a concrete floor. I've never done anything with concrete. They have that ready-mix, you just add water. It doesn't cost much."

Jeremy sighed. There went his allowance again. Kelly was going to keep practicing and practicing on the fort until probably it would have a bell tower like a church, and elevators and sliding doors and a bathtub and everything Kelly wanted to learn about. It would be forty stories high and camouflaged with pricker bushes clear up to the sky.

"We can't put cement on that dirt," he said. "It's all roots and rocks."

"We'll have to level it," said Kelly. "With the shovel."

More work. In the tank, Glatisant slid his head down under the leaves.

Two

OLIVER, ROSALIE'S BABY, sat in the highchair with applesauce all over his cheeks and watched her and Jeremy eat. Rosalie's eyes were pink from crying.

It was strange not to have their mother eating with them these days. It felt like an emergency that just went on and on, to have her chair empty all the time. No one home but the kids, Jeremy thought. Of course, now that she was married and had a baby, Rosalie wasn't exactly a kid, but she was still just his sister. Not the same as a real, experienced grownup. Suppose something happened, like the stove catching fire?

Since the divorce their mother worked in a place called a clinic, but not the kind you go to for a tetanus shot. It was a health clinic for people on special diets for their heart or their blood pressure. His mother's job was to welcome people when they came, and show them their rooms and where to go for the exercises, and drive them to the hairdresser or take their clothes to the cleaner or whatever else they wanted. Now that she worked evenings, too, she ran the movie projector and answered the phones and changed the records when the patients danced. She was always tired when she got home.

When they finished eating, Jeremy rinsed the dishes and put them in the dishwasher and Rosalie put the baby to bed.

In the living room Jeremy turned on the television.

"No TV on school nights," said Rosalie. She was writing in her black notebook. She'd write a word, and then think and suck on her pen, and then write some more.

"I don't have any homework." He did, but it was just a worksheet he could do on the bus in the morning.

"It's the rule," said Rosalie. "It was the rule for me and it's the rule for you. Why don't you read something?"

He turned off the television and got his book and shook it to see where it would fall open.

It was the story where King Arthur breaks his sword fighting with King Pellinore, and Merlin takes him to get a new one, and they follow the white deer and meet the lady in green. She blows a whistle made out of an emerald, and the brass boat comes zipping over and Arthur gets in, and it takes him to the middle of the lake where the lady's arm is sticking up out of the water holding a sword. So he takes the sword and goes back to fight King Pellinore again, and knocks him down to his knees, and then forgives him and gives him back his castle.

Jeremy settled down into the story. He'd read it so often it wasn't like reading at all, more like the page just walking in through his eyes and turning into a movie in his head. It must have been summer all the time in Round Table times, with striped tents in a big field for jousting, and thousands of pennants flying. Horses thundering past in silk blankets with embroidered headcovers and scalloped reins. Knights waiting at the shallow place in the stream to challenge the other knights going by. People had fun back then.

He wondered what Kelly would think of a brass boat that could float. Kelly hated made-up stories.

Rosalie got up and stretched and came and pushed his book back to look at the cover. "'King Arthur and his Knights of the Round Table,'" she read. "That looks familiar. You were reading that back before I went to college."

"Yeah, I guess so."

"Do you just keep reading it over and over?"

He didn't answer. Sometimes she did act like a grownup, or at least a kid playing grownup.

"I thought boys your age read about spaceships and computers and things like that."

"That's at school. We have to read all that stuff, science and all that, for school. This is just for fun."

"Do you want to be a knight when you grow up, Jerry?" she teased. "Gallop around rescuing maidens and killing dragons?"

"Don't be dumb. People don't do things like that anymore. You have to get just a plain job nowadays, and besides, there never were any real dragons. Do you think I'm retarded or something? I didn't say I believed this stuff. I just like to read about it."

"Okay, sorry. Go right ahead, be my guest. I'm going to bed."

"Aren't you waiting up for Mom?"

"I'm tired. Oliver got me up at six this morning."

"Rosalie? How long will it take for Mack to get here?" Jeremy rolled the corner of the page between his thumb and finger.

"I don't know how he's coming. I don't think he has much money."

"Doesn't he have a car?"

"He had a truck, but he wrecked it."

"He could get another one. Or he could fly. If he was flying he'd be here tomorrow."

"It costs a lot. Look, I don't want to talk about it. I have to get some sleep. 'Night." And she ran up the steps quietly so as not to wake the baby.

Jeremy finished reading about the sword Excalibur, and started the story where the wicked Queen Morgan le Fay gives Arthur a magic horse, and it whisks him off to the place where he gets kidnapped by twelve beautiful girls in a sailboat.

It was hard to pay attention, though. The house was too quiet. Without his watch he had to keep getting up to look at the clock in the kitchen. He tried turning the television on very low, so Rosalie wouldn't hear, but the only programs on were talk shows. He opened the book again. He felt as if he were waiting for something to happen.

The phone rang. Somehow he was sure it was Mack again.

He let it ring four times. He didn't want to talk to Mack. Maybe Rosalie would get it upstairs. On the fifth ring he picked it up, and heard the coins falling, *clang, clang* for the quarters and *ping* for the dimes, and the voice again. "Is Rosalie there?"

"She's gone to bed."

"Bed? What time is it there?"

"Past ten."

"You're sure she's in bed? You wouldn't be telling Mack a lie, would you, sonny?"

"Sure I'm sure."

"You're brother Jeremy, right? Okay, I've got a message for Rosie. You'll give her the message?"

"Of course."

"Here it is. I've got a van. It's a '72 but it runs all right. And I'm in Scotts Bluff, Nebraska. You got that? That's all you have to tell her. Say, 'Mack's in Scotts Bluff, Nebraska.' Got it? Good." And he hung up.

Jeremy went upstairs to Rosalie's room and pushed the door open on darkness. "Rosalie?" No answer. "Rosalie?"

"I'm asleep."

"That was Mack again. On the phone."

"I know."

"He said to tell you he's in Scotts Bluff, Nebraska."

"I don't even know where that is."

"And he has a van."

He heard the angry thrash of sheets as his sister rolled over and put the pillow over her head. "I'm not listening," she mumbled. "I'm asleep."

Downstairs in the dining-room bookcase there was a big atlas, with maps of everywhere. Jeremy hauled it out and opened it on the table.

There was the map of the whole United States, with Wyoming out in the West. Not as far west as California, but California was almost like a separate country. Wyoming was the real West. You could tell by the name, with the lonesome *o* sound in the middle like wind coming down the canyons. There'd be mountains with snow on their tops even in winter. Open range, with herds of sheep and a shepherd sitting on a horse and never seeing anyone to talk to for months on end. Just sheep. And coyotes.

Jeremy flipped past the other states to the Wyoming page. His school didn't teach much geography. Kids said that next year he'd have to memorize all the state capitals, but just their names, not anything about them.

The capital of Wyoming was Cheyenne. Sheridan, Wyoming, where Mack went to jail, was way up in the North, almost in Montana. Montana was flat up against Canada. Blizzards in the winter, probably, with the snow whipping across the valleys, and sheep and cattle buried in it.

Nebraska was east of Wyoming. Closer. It was almost in the middle of the country, not so much west at all or so lonely. The atlas said Wyoming had only about 300,000 people in it, but Nebraska had a million and a half. Mack had driven down from northern Wyoming and across to Nebraska. Jeremy thought about him in the '72 van, roaring and clattering along the empty straight roads of Wyoming, and the sun going down behind the Bighorn Mountains. Across Rawhide Creek and into Scotts Bluff. Scotts Bluff was on the North Platte River. Population: 14,507. Would they have a motel there? Or maybe he'd sleep in the van. Get up in the morning and maybe wash his face in the North Platte, if he was the kind of person who did wash his face, and keep on driving east.

The door opened and his mother came in.

"Jeremy, you're not still up? It's almost eleven, and I've told you over and over not to wait up for me on school nights." She leaned against the wall and took off her shoes and rubbed her stockinged feet. "You'll be a wreck in the morning. What are you doing with the atlas? You aren't going anywhere but to bed. Give me a kiss and scoot."

"*Mom.*"

"What, then? Make it quick."

"Mack's coming."

"Mack?"

"Rosalie's *husband.*"

"Oh, of course. I don't know where my head is. Coming here?"

"Coming to get Rosalie and the baby. He got out of jail and he's coming to get them and take them to Texas."

"Heavens, really? Oh dear, I'll miss having them, but I'm sure she's happy about it."

Jeremy closed the atlas. How come nobody else understood about Rosalie? Kelly, and his mother, and everyone thought she *meant* to be married to Mack.

They didn't understand how she could do things just to see how they felt, and not really mean them at all. Not seriously. She always did things just to try them, like the time she cut her hair off, or the time she and her friend Missy ran away. She never thought anything was for keeps.

"She's not happy," he said. "She was crying."

"Oh dear. Well, I'm sure she'll be glad to see him when he gets here. You know how she is."

He knew how she was. He wasn't sure his mother did, though.

"Now run along to bed. I'll be up in five minutes, and I want you asleep by then."

He went upstairs thinking that Kelly was right and it was none of his business. He wasn't the father around here.

Just the same, he was glad it was Rosalie that Mack was coming for and not him. There was something about his voice on the phone that Jeremy definitely didn't like.

Three

THE NEXT DAY was Thursday, one of his mother's early days, so Jeremy got his own breakfast and packed his own lunch.

At school he told his friend Kevin about Mack. Kevin was his best friend, in a way, but they hardly ever saw each other except at school, because Kevin lived on the far opposite side of the school district. It was a long trip even when Jeremy's bike was working, which it hadn't done since he took it apart a couple of months ago.

Kevin thought he was right to be worried. "He might be crazy, this Mack. He sounds kind of crazy. He might have a gun, people have guns a lot out there. Just hope he comes when you're not there."

"What about Rosalie and the baby?"

"That's *their* worry. It's dumb to go off with a baby if you don't have any money or a job. People like us can live on pizza or something, but babies need a lot of stuff like orange juice." Kevin had twin baby brothers and knew all about them. "And where would they sleep?"

"In the van, I guess," said Jeremy.

"And what if he doesn't get a job? If you ask me, this dude's either dumb or more likely crazy. You'd better stay away from him."

After school it was raining too hard to work on the fort, so Jeremy stayed home and ate some leftover ice cream and played with the baby. Oliver was just learning to crawl, and Jeremy crawled after him on his hands and knees, and the baby would shriek and try to crawl faster until his knees flew out from under him and he fell down flat, laughing. It was a pretty childish game, and Jeremy was glad there was no one from school to see him. But Oliver wasn't bad, for a baby. Jeremy could always get a laugh out of him, and besides, he was his uncle.

"Uncle" sounded very old, older even than "father," for some reason. Jeremy tried to imagine himself that old, but all he could see was himself taller. The same Jeremy, but with stretched-out legs and his own face perched on top. He tried to put a beard on this person, but it looked like a Halloween beard. He was probably boring, this Jeremy, and worked in an office. If you weren't super-smart like Rosalie or a computer whiz like Kevin or a builder like Kelly, or even good at fixing broken things, that's what you did. You sat at a desk.

"Watch Oliver," said Rosalie. "He's after the lamp cord."

Jeremy pulled him, shrieking, away from the cord and plunked him down in his highchair and gave him a pan and a spoon to bang with.

Rosalie moved her notebook out of reach and went on writing.

"Da, da, da, da!" said Oliver.

"Is he trying to say 'daddy'?" asked Jeremy.

Rosalie frowned at her book.

"Daddy," said Jeremy to Oliver. "Dad-dy. Dad-dy."

"Shut up," said Rosalie, and put her pen down. "Mam-ma," she said.

"Ba, ba, ba," said Oliver.

Rosalie laughed, and started to do creepy-mouse. She walked her fingers across the table toward the baby, very slowly. The baby watched. "Creeeeepy-mouse coming to get you," whispered Rosalie. "Creeeeepy-mouse coming to get you." Walk, walk went the fingers. Oliver sat frozen. "Mom used to do this to you, Jeremy. I guess she did it to me too. Creeepy-mouse coming to get you." The fingers walked closer. Closer. The baby stared at them. "Creepy-mouse coming to . . . *get you!*"

And the fingers leaped forward and grabbed Oliver in the stomach and tickled him while he screamed with joy and relief.

The phone rang.

Rosalie and Jeremy stared at each other.

"You get it," said Rosalie.

"It's for you."

"If it's for me, I'm not here."

"He'll be mad."

"He'll be madder if you don't answer it."

Jeremy picked it up and said "Hello?" and then had to clear his throat and say it again.

The coins banged down. The voice said, "She better not be asleep this time."

"You mean Rosalie?" He could feel his heart thumping in his ears. "She's not here."

"What do you mean, not here? She go out with someone?"

"No. I mean, not with someone. Just out."

"Out where?"

Jeremy scrabbled in his head for an answer. It was hard enough to think up lies when you were alone and had plenty of time, but when you were nervous and in a hurry, your mind just went dead. Where did people go when they went out?

"I guess you didn't hear me, sonny. I said, out where?"

"To the grocery store!" Jeremy cried, almost shouting in triumph.

There was a pause, and then the voice said, "Sonny, I really hope you aren't lying to Mack. I really hope so." He sounded sad, and so quiet Jeremy could hardly hear him.

Rosalie sat across the room at the table. Nobody can see through a telephone; telephones are strictly sound only. Just the same Jeremy hunched himself closer to the phone, blocking out its view of the room. "She had to buy some groceries," he said, like an idiot. What else would you buy at the grocery store — ice skates?

"I believe you this time," said the voice softly. "Mack likes to trust people. I believed you last night. But twice is enough, okay? Now listen. I know she's real anxious to find out where I am. So you give her this message. Tell her I'm in Lincoln. Lincoln, Nebraska. Got it?" And he hung up.

"He's still only in Nebraska," said Jeremy. Mack had been in the same state since yesterday, almost as if he hadn't moved at all. Just been driving and driving beside the same cattle or the same stalks of corn all day.

He got out the atlas and opened it to Nebraska.

No. Mack hadn't been standing still. He'd gone clear across a big state, from Scotts Bluff in the far west to Lincoln in the east.

"Lincoln is the capital of Nebraska," he said.

"Big whoop," said Rosalie.

"Nebraska produces corn, hogs, wheat, and sorghums." That was tame country, like a vegetable garden, compared to Wyoming. In Nebraska people planted things and then went out and got them and brought them home and sold them. In Wyoming, you just sent the sheep and cattle out to eat whatever was there. That was the real West. "What are sorghums?"

"How should I know?"

"Well, you were out there. Out West. I thought you might have seen some."

"All I saw was the inside of a trailer in a trailer park. Mack's mother and stepfather sat in there all day long and played gin rummy and drank diet soda. I sat there and waited for Oliver to be born, and then I sat there and took care of him."

"What about before? In college?"

"College was like a college. They didn't have sorghums. Jerry, do you want to hear a poem?"

"You know I don't understand the stuff you write."

"This one's easy. Listen.

Whom have we loved? O clear, how green
Runs the day's flesh along the seaward tide
Where all the channel bells cry lost, and lost."

"Easy?"
"Wait.

Passing a famous bridge, dismantled by —"

"What's 'dismantled'?"
"Taken apart.

dismantled by
War perhaps, or time only, its arches
Broken and wading to their granite knees —"

"Rosalie? What did you want to marry a freak like Mack for anyway?"

She looked up from her book, past Jeremy at the wall. "He looked so great. Light-colored eyes, as if he was looking at mountains all the time. I thought he was a real man, like in the movies. I was an awful idiot. He drove an old blue pickup truck, but I always thought of him on horseback. Loping along singing."

"You know what?" said Jeremy. "You ought to be locked up in a rubber room. You can't marry people because they're like a cowboy in a movie. And *now* look what's happening."

They both turned toward the phone as if it might be ringing.

"I'm sorry," said Rosalie. "Boy, am I ever sorry."

"Fat lot of good that does. And you're supposed to be the one that's so smart. What are you going to do when he gets here?"

"I don't know. I can't think."

"You'd better think. He's getting closer all the time."

"Creepy-mouse coming to get me," said Rosalie, and Jeremy thought it was a joke, but she looked so scared he didn't laugh.

Four

THE NEXT DAY, when Jeremy got home from school, a strange noise greeted him from the kitchen. He walked in carefully, holding his books up against his chest for protection, and looked around. It took him a minute to find the sound. The telephone receiver was hanging down against the wall, dangling on its curly cord and squawking. Rosalie must have taken it off the hook.

He lifted the receiver up by the cord as if it might be hot and put it back. It shut up.

Mack must have called while he was in school. Rosalie probably just picked the phone up and dropped it, and left it hanging there with Mack shouting "Hello? Hello?" while she walked away.

In the silence Jeremy could hear her upstairs singing to the baby.

It might ring again at any minute. Jeremy dropped his books on the table and got an apple and went over to Kelly's.

Kelly's house was more ordinary than his own, with a father, and a mother who didn't work and stayed home to fuss about things like floor wax and whether Kelly took her vitamins. Nobody in Kelly's house went to jail or wrote poetry or anything weird at all. You always knew what was going to happen, because it was always the same things, which was kind of peaceful.

Jeremy remembered to wipe his feet when he went in. You wiped your feet at Kelly's house even when they weren't muddy.

Kelly was up in her room hammering. She was building a frame, only she called it a form, to pour cement into for the floor of the fort.

Kelly's room was bare. Her mother used to bother her all the time about keeping it neat, so one day she got mad and threw everything away. She got a lot of trash bags and filled them with her old stuffed animals and model planes and Matchbox cars and her posters and the sheepskin rug and the cactus collection and the beer can collection and her swimming trophies and all her books except one called *The Home Building Manual*. She even threw out a lot of her clothes.

That was Kelly for you. She made up her mind fast, and nothing stopped her. Jeremy was never quite sure just when his own mind was made up; other people always seemed to get theirs made up first and push him along with their plans. Like slapjack, the fastest people always won. Look at Mack and the way he decided to come get Rosalie and just hopped in a van and started driving. Nobody could stop him, either.

Kelly looked up from her hammering. "Mom found Glassident," she said.

"Glatisant? Was she mad?"

"Yeah, She said snakes were dirty. I told her they only eat about twice a week, so they don't go to the bathroom much, but she said to get him out anyway."

"She didn't hurt him?"

"Mom? She wouldn't touch him with the end of a broom. You should have heard her holler. You know how funny people are about snakes. We better take him back to the hut."

"Did he eat the hamburger?"

"I guess so. I can't find it. Hold this flat while I nail it."

"I don't see what we need a cement floor for anyway," Jeremy objected. "The dirt's just as comfortable. Cement's scratchy." The truth was, he was bored with the fort, and the way Kelly got to have all the ideas and he just got to help with the work.

"Ours won't be scratchy," she said. "We'll level it with a strike board and then trowel it smooth. See?"

She pointed to some pictures in *The Home Building Manual*, open beside her on the floor, of a man's arms doing different things with cement. They were very boring pictures. "That's why the form has to be level across the top." She laid the spirit level on a corner and frowned at it. "For the strike board," she explained. "See?"

Jeremy didn't, but he didn't want to be told, either, so he nodded. All he could think of was the phone in the kitchen dangling and squawking. If Mack was angry before, how would he feel now?

"You don't have a steel trowel, do you?" asked Kelly.

"Are you kidding?"

"I thought you might. Your mother got you that awesome tool kit for Christmas, so you could fix stuff around the house."

"There aren't any trowels in it." At least, he didn't think there were. There might be. The kit was full of strange things he didn't recognize. He hadn't fixed anything with it yet, either. The sink dripped worse now than before he worked on it.

When Kelly had finished the form, he helped her sand the inside smooth, and then they went downstairs.

Kelly's father was home already, and sitting in his chair. Even when he was away at his office, nobody else ever sat in Mr. Flynn's chair. It was an ordinary armchair in a purplish color, but it was his, and now he sat there reading his paper.

Probably I'll have a chair when I grow up, thought Jeremy. That will be me, reading the paper. He tried to imagine himself as an accountant like Mr. Flynn, adding up money all day, but he was getting a C minus in math, so it wasn't likely. He'd have to think of something else.

It would be manners to say good evening, but Mr. Flynn didn't look as if he noticed him, or Kelly either, so the two of them went on past him and down to the basement for Glatisant.

"He'll like it better in the fort," said Jeremy. "Fresh air. And it's spring now."

Kelly swiped two hot dogs from the refrigerator, and they took turns carrying the tank down Church Street, and the two blocks down Spring Street to Maple, and through the thin, brambly woods to the hut. Confused by the motion, Glatisant kept feeling the glass walls with his head.

They put some crumbs of hot dog in his tank and went back to their own houses.

Coming up the walk, Jeremy could hear the phone ringing inside the house. Nobody seemed to be answering it.

He stopped and thought about going over to Kelly's again. But the Flynns ate dinner early, and Kelly's mother was strict about people not hanging around unless they were invited, which they mostly weren't.

Then he thought about just standing there until the phone stopped ringing, but it didn't sound as if it would ever stop.

In the kitchen Rosalie was getting the baby's dinner, moving around the kitchen with her face as blank as if she were deaf, and the baby sat in his highchair and cried, and the phone rang and rang.

"Aren't you going to answer it?" shouted Jeremy.

"No."

"Maybe it's somebody else. Maybe it's Kevin, or Mom."

"I don't care. Please be quiet, Oliver, you're driving me nuts."

"Suppose it's Mom and it's an emergency?"

"Answer it, then. If it isn't Mom you can hang up."

He picked it up and held it a little away from his ear. "Hello?" he whispered.

The coins fell down.

"Hang up," hissed Rosalie. She picked Oliver up and hushed him against her shoulder.

If he hung up it would make it worse the next time.

"Hello, sonny," said the voice. "Was that you playing a little joke on Mack this afternoon? When I called from Davenport?"

"Davenport?" said Jeremy. "No, it wasn't me. Honest."

"Sure it was. Just took the phone off the hook, huh? Maybe you better tell me, nicely now, why you won't let me talk to your sister. You think Mack's not good enough for her?"

"No, of course not. It wasn't me. She doesn't –" And he stopped himself.

"Doesn't what? Don't try to tell me my little wife doesn't want to talk to me. All the girls like to talk to Mack, and Rosie's my wife, isn't she? Isn't she?"

Jeremy looked over his shoulder for help, but Rosalie had her back to him, her shoulders hunched up to her ears. He couldn't think of the right thing to say.

"It looks like, when I get there, I'm going to have to explain some things to you, sonny. Have a nice little talk, just you and Mack, so you understand some things. Like about playing jokes on old Mack. Right?"

"Sure," said Jeremy, and it came out in a squeak.

Mack's voice got soft and quiet again. "We can't have you thinking there's something wrong with old Mack, just because he didn't go to some fancy college like your sister," he said. "After all, we're brothers, right?"

"I guess so."

"Sure we are. So we'll just have a little talk when I get there, and then we'll be real buddies. Now you go find Rosalie and you give her this message, okay? Because she'd be real sad if she didn't get my messages. Say, 'Mack's in Normal, Illinois.'"

"Illinois?"

"Not too sharp, are you? Normal, Illinois. Outside Bloomington." And the phone clicked off.

Illinois? What happened to Iowa? How did he get clear across Iowa?

"He's in Normal, Illinois," said Jeremy.

"There's no such place," said Rosalie, and sat down to spoon oatmeal into Oliver. "There can't be. He's probably still in Sheridan, Wyoming, and making the whole thing up. Just to scare me."

Jeremy looked up Iowa. It was big and square and flat, and full of corn and pigs and cows. Farms. Huge, flat farms, probably, with enormous machinery. Probably people drove machines like giant prehistoric bugs back and forth in the fields. Maybe all night long, clattering and roaring, with the headlight eyes crawling along in the dark miles of corn.

Mack had driven straight across it and out of it in a day, in a beat-up old van that probably wouldn't do more than fifty without shaking itself to bits. He said he'd called from Davenport before, when Rosalie took the phone off. Davenport was in Iowa, in the east of it, on the closer edge. On the Mississippi River.

He'd crossed the Mississippi. Even Jeremy had heard about that, the great river that poured down through the middle of the country and separated the East from the West. Now he was in the East. Illinois.

Illinois was so scribbled over with towns and cities

that he couldn't find Normal. The atlas said Illinois produced soybeans and hogs and corn and oats, but he didn't see how there was space enough between the towns to grow anything, even a flower. Up in one corner was Chicago, on Lake Michigan. He'd heard of that too.

"Ba, ba!" said Oliver, and dribbled oatmeal.

"He crossed the Mississippi," said Jeremy.

"Hurray for him. I wish he'd fallen in."

"And now he's mad at me, too. He thinks I won't let him talk to you."

"Oh, Jerry." She looked up, Oliver's spoon forgotten in her hand. "I'm sorry. I shouldn't have done that to you."

"Rosalie? Maybe you're wrong about him? I mean, maybe he's not so bad? After all, he didn't even really hit that policeman, he just tried to."

"That wasn't the first time Mack went to jail." Oliver grabbed for the spoon and got oatmeal in his eye, and Rosalie wiped him off with a dish towel. "He did thirty days before, for fighting. In a bar, with a knife."

"Oh. Well, maybe the other guy started it. Maybe Mack really wants to be nice, and just can't help sounding scary. Maybe he wants to be friends."

"I don't think so. He doesn't have any friends. He was friends with his brother for a while, but that was before the trouble with the chain saw."

"What chain saw?"

"They were cutting firewood to sell, Mack and his brother. That's what he did for money, before he wrecked the truck. It wasn't their wood, it was government land, part of a national forest, but they had a secret way in and out of it." She scraped oatmeal off Oliver's chin and poked it back into his mouth. "His brother was teasing him about something, and Mack got mad and chased him with the chain saw. His brother said it was so close it ripped the leather jacket off his back and chewed it to shreds. He said Mack was crazy, and he moved to Colorado."

"A chain saw. Wow. Did you tell Mom?"

"No. She doesn't listen to things like that. She wouldn't even believe it. She likes to think everyone's happy and nice."

Jeremy hadn't thought about that before, but it was true. Back in third grade he used to come home complaining about the fifth-grade bullies, and Mom always said they couldn't be that bad. She said if he'd smile and be friendly with the bullies, then they'd be friendly too. But of course it didn't work.

Mack didn't sound as if smiling would work with him either.

Five

THE NEXT DAY was Saturday. Rosalie put the baby in the stroller and went for a walk, and Jeremy's mother went out to do her week's errands and shopping, and get her hair cut. She had to look nice for her job, and spent a lot of money on haircuts and clothes.

Jeremy settled at the kitchen table to read about Sir Tristram taking Iseult the Fair back to Cornwall to marry his uncle, and how Sir Brewnor captured them and held them prisoner in his castle, and Tristram had to chop off his head. Then Sir Galahalte the High Prince and the King of the Hundred Knights came galloping up to avenge Sir Brewnor. But all the time Jeremy kept hearing the van, Mack's van, wheezing and rattling across Illinois toward Ohio. The noise seemed to be getting louder as he got closer. Louder than the Hundred Knights galloping in full armor.

What could Mack actually do to them? He couldn't really kill them, after all. That only happens in stories, or on television. Real people don't kill people.

Crazy people do, his head answered. Crazy people don't know what they're doing. Kevin said they did things like biting the heads off of rats. Maybe Mack was crazy.

But that was stupid. He was making it up, scaring himself like little kids telling ghost stories. Even if Mack was crazy, it was Rosalie he was really after. He wouldn't do much to Jeremy except maybe hit him, and how badly could it hurt, getting hit? In a few days he'd feel better and it would all be over.

Poor Rosalie, though. Poor Oliver. Jeremy thought of Texas, and how big it was. Everywhere you looked there'd be all that sky. Desert reaching clear to the edge of the sky, and nothing in it but maybe a single trailer home like a dot in all that flat space, and Rosalie and Oliver trapped inside it.

It was her own fault, of course. She should have had better sense than to get mixed up with crazies.

It wasn't the baby's own fault, though.

Jeremy punched his head. There wasn't anything he could do, so it was dumb to sit and worry. He got some peanuts and a couple of apples and the crumbs in the bottom of the cookie box and went back to his book.

He turned to where the knight on the black horse snatches up the lady and carries her off screaming, and Sir Gawaine takes off after them, and fights with Sir Alardin of the Isles.

It used to be more exciting to be good. These days, being good meant wimpy things like getting A's on your report card or cleaning up your room. For grownups, maybe just giving quarters to bums on the street, which was okay probably but not much fun. Not like rescuing people and whacking wicked knights with your sword.

Jeremy munched, and read, and the electric clock purred over the stove.

When the phone rang he jumped so hard he banged his knee on the table and scattered peanut shells all over.

No, he thought. Please, no. Just let me go on reading.

He let it ring six times, and then thought, it feels worse waiting to answer it than answering it, so he picked it up.

It was Kelly, saying she had the concrete mix for the floor of the fort. "Your brother-in-law get there yet?" she asked.

"No, he's in Illinois or Indiana. Or maybe even in Ohio by now."

"Maybe his car will break down."

"It's a van. An old van. If it did, he'd probably just get another one."

"Steal one, do you think?"

"Yeah. Listen, I'll come help you carry the stuff. What are we going to mix it in?" Today it sounded good, working on the fort. The safe secret fort with no telephones in it. Jeremy barely stopped long enough to stuff the last cookie bits into his pockets and scribble a note saying where he was, and left the house as if it were on fire.

They had to pull the concrete bag over in Kelly's brother's red wagon, and Kelly was afraid people would notice, or even follow them. "Just look businesslike," said Jeremy.

Kelly tried to look businesslike, but it came out looking cross. She and Jeremy took turns pulling the wagon and carrying Mrs. Flynn's scrub bucket full of water, which slopped badly.

When they got to the woods, the wagon wouldn't go in through the bushes and trees and rocks, so they had to drag the concrete mix the rest of the way. It was heavy and hard to get a grip on.

Glatisant hadn't eaten his bits of hot dog. He lay very still, and you had to look closely to see his sides move in and out as he breathed. "I don't think snakes like hot dogs," said Jeremy. "We ought to get him some mice." They carried his tank outside so they could work on the floor.

They mixed the concrete in batches in the wagon and spooned it into the frame with a trowel, being

42

careful of air pockets. Kelly leveled it off with the side of a yardstick, to make it smooth. It looked like a square of new sidewalk.

"We ought to season it," she said. "That makes it stronger."

"It doesn't need to be any stronger."

"I guess not." She seemed sad that there wasn't any more to do, and peered around the dark inside of the fort. "There's still a lot of cement left. I wonder if it would be hard to make a chimney."

"You're kidding. For a fire? People would see the smoke, and they'd have the fire department here before you could sneeze."

"There ought to be something, though." She gazed at the rest of the concrete, thinking of what to build.

Jeremy took a stick and wrote across one corner of the new floor, in small letters and very neatly, "Sir Jeremy the Black Knight of the Lake was here."

He was almost finished before Kelly noticed and started to yell. "Look what you've done! I had it so smooth, and you've ruined it!"

He finished with a curly flourish and handed her the stick. "Here, put your name in it too. Why not? It doesn't spoil it, it shows it's ours. We made it."

Kelly threw the stick into the bushes. "You just don't understand. That's what kids do, playing. This isn't a game, it's my *job*."

Her job. She was always saying things like that, and it made Jeremy feel about two years old.

"It's my fort too," he said. "I did half the work."

"You wouldn't know what to do if I didn't show you. If you'd built it yourself it would have fallen down by now."

"Just because you built it, you think it can't fall down? Watch this!" Jeremy grabbed the pole at the side of the doorway and shook it as hard as he could, and the fort swayed.

"Stop it!" Kelly tried to pull him away, but he twisted her off and kept rocking. She backed off and ran at him, and butted him full-tilt in the stomach with her head. It knocked the wind out of him and threw him backward into a blackberry bush.

Kelly stood breathing hard and glaring at him with her face red.

He got up carefully, untangling his jacket from the thorns. He ought to punch her. Just walk over and knock her down, but you weren't supposed to hit girls. Besides, it wouldn't be all that easy.

"What did you do that for?" he panted. "You could have broken my ribs. Maybe you did."

"You tried to pull the hut down."

"I wasn't really going to. What do you think I am?"

She thought about that, and then said, "I think you're silly."

"*You* think you're some kind of boss. You can't be a builder. You think real workmen are going to listen to a girl? I'm going home."

"What about all the stuff?"

"Take it back yourself. It's yours, isn't it?" And he pushed his way out toward the street. He noticed they'd left a trail, dragging the concrete bag, and as he went he kicked leaves back over it to hide it.

When he got home his mother was in the kitchen making a meat loaf, and she complained when she saw his clothes. They were flecked with little gray splashes of cement. She said he even had cement in his eyebrows.

Jeremy got out the atlas and sat down. Mack would surely be in Ohio by now, still following his long straight line toward this house. They all just sat still, Jeremy and Rosalie and Oliver, while Mack kept moving toward them. What would he do when he got there? That was for him to decide, and all they could do was wait and find out.

Rosalie was feeding the baby, singing one of her nonsense songs to him. Jeremy's stomach hurt from Kelly's head. He flipped through the pages, killing time. Waiting. He found a map of different places where American Indians used to live, and whispered their tribal names to himself: Iroquois, Micmac, Nanticoke, Arapaho, Yaquina. They sounded like the names of mountains.

The phone rang, and Jeremy hunched down over the book. Rosalie picked Oliver up and jiggled him on her shoulder.

"Isn't anyone going to answer that?" asked her mother. She was slapping the meat loaf into shape.

"I'm busy," said Jeremy.

Rosalie ducked her head down beside the baby, and her yellow braids fell forward. She didn't say anything. The phone went on ringing.

"What's the matter with you two?" said their mother crossly. "Jeremy, I believe you're getting as silly as your sister." She wiped her sticky hands on a dish towel and picked up the phone. "Hello?"

Jeremy could hear the coins clanging down. I will hate that noise all my life, he thought.

"Hello?" she said again, and then, "Oh, hello! I'm Rosalie's mother. . . . Yes, so I heard. It'll be very nice to meet you. Are you enjoying your trip? . . . Yes, I'm taking good care of her for you. She's fine. . . . Of course, I'll give her the message. See you soon, then. Goodbye."

She hung up and said, "Mack certainly sounds friendly and nice, Rosalie. Very polite, very nice manners. After all, lots of young people make mistakes, and we mustn't be too hard on them."

"Mother, it isn't that," cried Rosalie. "It isn't what he did. I just don't want to go off alone with him. I'm scared."

"I'm sure you're getting yourself all in a fuss for nothing, sweetie. But we'll know more when we see him. Oh, and he said to tell you he's in Columbus, Ohio."

She went back to the meat loaf, and Rosalie carried Oliver up to bed without answering.

Jeremy turned to Ohio in the atlas.

It was crowded. There were ten and a half million people in the state. Back in Wyoming you could probably drive all day and not see anyone at all. The farther east you got, the thicker the people got. They were like peanut butter you spread on bread. In Ohio it would be too thick to swallow, while out in Wyoming and Montana there'd be hardly enough to taste.

"You know what they make in Ohio?" Jeremy asked his mother, and she made the "Mmm" sound that meant she wasn't listening. "Machinery, electrical and metal products, business machines, refrigerators, rubber goods, aircraft parts, paper products —"

"Don't you have any homework?"

"It's Saturday. Machine tools, safes, transportation equipment, chemicals, soap, printing, paint, trucks, glass, roller bearings, vacuum cleaners —"

"Is this for Social Studies?"

"No."

Lake Erie ran across the top of Ohio. Mack was in Columbus, down toward the middle. On the eastern edge of the state was Pennsylvania. The state where Jeremy was sitting, here in the kitchen.

Creepy-mouse coming to get you.

He slammed the atlas shut and went to turn on the television, but there was nothing but old cartoons he'd seen a hundred times.

He went upstairs and stood in the door of Rosalie's room. She went on singing, leaning over the edge of the baby's crib. She sang:

> *Softer than dandelions,*
> *Cooler than silk.*
> *Newer than baby lambs*
> *Newer than milk.*

If I were Rosalie I wouldn't sing, Jeremy thought, I would run. Just wrap the baby up in something and start running.

It might be a good idea for him to run too. He thought of both of them running down the street with the baby, and the van coming after them and getting closer and closer, with its headlights like big white eyes.

And even if they got away, Mack would find them. If you could track people down all the way from Sheridan, Wyoming, you could find them anywhere.

Six

ALL DAY SUNDAY the phone kept ringing. Jeremy's Aunt Sheila called to ask after Rosalie and the baby. A woman called wanting them to subscribe to the *Evening Standard*. A man called wanting to talk to Charlotte, and refused to believe he'd called the wrong number. Jeremy's mother's friend Eleanor called just to talk. Kelly called and said she was sorry about yesterday, and maybe they should try making concrete steps. Jeremy said it was all right about yesterday, but steps sounded too hard. Rosalie's friend Missy called to talk about her boyfriend, and a man called wanting them to buy aluminum siding, and Kevin called to ask what the English homework was.

Every time the phone rang, Jeremy was sure it was Mack . . . but it wasn't.

They had a late breakfast, with pancakes, and then Jeremy made himself some cheese-and-tomato sandwiches for lunch, and Rosalie wrote in her little book, and his mother read the Sunday paper. The day went by, and the evening, and Jeremy kept on waiting.

His mother went upstairs to soak in a hot bath. Sunday was the only night she had time for a real bath.

Rosalie and Jeremy rinsed the supper dishes and loaded the dishwasher, and Rosalie, who never broke anything, broke a glass and cut her hand on the pieces. Jeremy dropped a plate.

"Maybe he's changed his mind," he said, dumping the two pieces of plate in the trash. "Maybe he turned around and went back West."

"I don't think so," said Rosalie. She was trying to get a Band-Aid to stick to her wet finger. "Nobody drives all the way from Wyoming to Ohio and then just says, 'Oh nuts,' and turns around and goes back."

"Why hasn't he called, then?"

"I don't know." She glared at the telephone as if there must be something wrong with it. "Maybe he ran out of change." She giggled nervously.

"It's worse not knowing," said Jeremy. "I mean, maybe he's almost here. Maybe he's so close he figured there's no sense calling, he could just walk in and surprise us. In the night, maybe."

"Yes, he could do that." She was whispering, as if

Mack might already be listening at the door. Then she straightened her shoulders and said, "I'm going to call the police."

"The *police*?"

"Why not? Isn't that what they're for? To protect people?" She marched over to the phone and dialed the police emergency number they kept pasted to the phone, along with the fire department and the rescue squad. It rang a long time before someone answered.

Jeremy kept rinsing the same fork over and over, and listened while Rosalie tried to explain what was happening. She didn't seem to be having much luck. Finally she said, "I'm *terribly* sorry if I bothered you," and hung up hard.

"What did they say?"

"They said no." She imitated a deep, serious voice, and said, "'You say your husband's coming to visit and you don't want to see him? That's *your* problem, lady. We're not marriage counselors. No law against visiting your wife.' They also said that number's for emergencies only."

"And they won't help."

"No." She sat down and started scraping crumbs into a pile on the table. "I guess there's not much they could do anyway. If they came, and Mack was here, he'd just talk nicely to them until they went away. You can't exactly ask the police force to move into your house and sit there for the rest of your life."

"There ought to be somebody," said Jeremy. What he meant was, We're just kids. Somebody ought to take care of us. But Rosalie wasn't a real kid anymore. What she needed was Sir Launcelot to sweep her and Oliver up on the back of his horse and gallop them off to his castle, the Joyous Gard, and keep them safe while he went back and chopped off Mack's head. Of course there weren't any knights now and probably there never had been, but it was too bad. It was about the only thing he could think of to help Rosalie.

They finished the dishes and fussed around the kitchen. They brushed the crumbs off the table and wiped down the stove and waited for the phone to ring, but it didn't.

They went to bed not knowing where Mack was.

Jeremy didn't sleep well. He had one dream where Mack was chasing him with a sword and laughing, and another dream where he was hiding in a tree and it started to shake and he realized Mack was cutting it down with a chain saw, and then a dream about the baby that was so awful and disgusting he forgot everything about it as soon as it woke him up.

It was still dark. He lay stiff in bed, listening to the house. There was a sound, a small sound, a kind of tapping and scratching. Not the sound of someone coming upstairs. Maybe someone at his bedroom door, though. Scratching and tapping.

He turned on the light by the bed, and then thought, No, that's the worst thing. He almost knocked it over turning it off again. If Mack were somewhere around he'd see it. He'd know Jeremy was awake. He had to pretend to be asleep. Lie still and make his breathing sound like a sleeping person's.

The tapping went on.

Of course. It was the wire that came down from the television aerial, past his window. It scratched on the pane when the wind blew. That was all.

A cough came from Rosalie's room. She was awake too.

Mack was somewhere out in the black night that covered the whole country, but not in the house. Not yet. Everything was safe for now.

Just the same it took him a long time to get back to sleep.

In the morning it was Monday, with the usual rushing around, and everyone wanting the bathroom, and Jeremy trying to make lunch and eat breakfast at the same time, and the radio blaring away with news and weather. His mother, looking important in her high-heeled shoes and suit, kissed them all goodbye and went to work. Oliver blew his oatmeal all over the table, and Rosalie called him a slob.

It was ten after eight, almost time for the school bus, when the phone rang. Jeremy picked it up quickly, on the second ring. He had to know. It was scary not knowing.

The coins clanged. Not so many coins now as before. "Hello," said Jeremy.

"Bet you were worried about me yesterday, weren't you?" said Mack.

"Yes," said Jeremy. It was true, in a way.

"Rosie must've been real upset too. Just a little trouble with the van, that's all. Had to stop and get it fixed in Wheeling. Wheeling, West Virginia. Got that?"

West Virginia? But that was down south, wasn't it? Was Mack *lost*? A wild hope jumped up in Jeremy, just for a second, of Mack missing his course entirely. Somehow missing the whole state of Pennsylvania and sliding off to the south, down through Virginia and North and South Carolina. Clear to the ocean. But that was silly, nobody could get that lost.

"So it looks like everything's okay now, and I'll be there sometime late today."

Today.

"What's the matter? Cat got your tongue? Now be sure to tell Rosalie, hear? Tell her I want her to put on a pretty dress for me. A dress like she wears for those other guys she goes out with."

"She doesn't. She doesn't go out."

"We'll see about that. One thing's sure, she won't be doing it anymore. And I hope you're not lying to Mack. Boys that tell lies get punished."

"I'm not."

"How's that kid of mine? His mamma spoiling him?" Mack grunted. "Calling him Oliver, that's as bad as Jeremy. You can't trust a woman to raise a boy. He's going to need some toughening."

Jeremy looked over at Oliver in his highchair and almost remembered the dream. Oliver looked little and soft. The dream had been disgusting. Too gruesome to remember.

"Don't have much to say, do you?" asked Mack.

"I have to catch the school bus," said Jeremy, and his voice was a whine, like begging.

" 'Have to catch the school bus,' " Mack imitated his whine, and laughed.

The operator said, "Do you wish an additional three minutes?" and Mack said, "I'm going to hit the road now. You wait there for me, hear?" and hung up.

"He's coming today," said Jeremy.

Maybe he'd be in school. Maybe Mack would come while he was in school, and be gone again when he got home. Of course, Rosalie and Oliver would be gone too.

"Where is he?" Rosalie asked.

"Wheeling, West Virginia."

"That's still a long way. Maybe he'll have an accident or something. At least he's not right outside." She looked out the window and said, "There goes the school bus. You missed it."

Seven

His lunch sat on the table, a brown paper bag with a peanut-butter sandwich and an apple in it. There was something gloomy about a school lunch to eat at home because you weren't going to school. And he wanted to go to school, badly. No one could hurt you too seriously at school. It was against the rules.

"I could walk," he said. "I'd miss Social Studies. Maybe part of Science."

"Stay here," said Rosalie. "Please stay here. I'll explain to Mother, she'll write you a note."

"You're the one that married him. I'd kind of like to not be here when he comes."

"I know." She looked very young, younger than Kelly, and he noticed she was biting her fingernails again the way she used to. "I just don't want to be alone with him."

Far down inside his ears he could hear the rattle of Mack's van coming across the state.

He got out the atlas again and found West Virginia. Yes, it was to the south, most of it, but for some crazy reason a thin finger of it poked up north in between Ohio and Pennsylvania, and that was where Wheeling was. On the Ohio River. Maybe it was terrible country that the two big states didn't want, and they'd made West Virginia take it even if it didn't fit right.

Wheeling. It sounded ugly, or maybe that was just because Mack was there. The atlas said Wheeling made iron and steel, chemicals, metal products. Probably they'd gotten the Ohio River all black and slimy with stuff from the factories. Probably in Wheeling it was always six o'clock in the evening and wintertime, with flames shooting out of factory chimneys and shining on the black smelly river, and a cold wind full of dirt.

Wheeling was only about thirty miles west of Pennsylvania.

He slammed the atlas shut and put it back in the bookcase. He put it in backward, with the pages facing out, and stuck some magazines in front of it, so he wouldn't have to see it again for years.

The day stretched out ahead with nothing to do but wait for Mack.

He felt as if he'd been waiting for Mack all his life.

He watched a game show on television until Rosalie said it made her nervous and he had to turn it off.

He found a banana in the kitchen marked, in ballpoint, "Oliver's banana — do not eat!" and ate it.

Rosalie folded the laundry and emptied the dishwasher. The mailman came, and Jeremy read a long letter that began, "You may already be a winner!" He never was, though. Come to think of it, he'd never won anything, not even a spelling bee.

Oliver woke up from his morning nap, and Rosalie brought him down and changed his diaper on the couch. Jeremy kept going to look out the windows, first one window and then another.

"What time do you think he'll get here?" he asked.

"How should I know?"

"Listen, Rosalie. Suppose when he gets here we just lock the doors? Don't let him in?"

She put Oliver into his backpack and pushed her arms through the straps. "What good would that do? He'd just wait. We can't stay in the house forever."

"It'd be like a siege," Jeremy said. "There were sieges in King Arthur times. They just camped around outside the castle till the people inside it starved."

"Yes, like that. Only Mother would come home and let him in. She doesn't understand." Rosalie chewed on her thumbnail.

"Da!" cried Oliver, and bounced up and down in his backpack.

Somewhere in their own state of Pennsylvania by now Mack was rattling closer in his van. Pittsburgh, Harrisburg, Lebanon, Lancaster, places like that. The steep hills of the coal country, and then the soft valleys full of wheat. Places so close even Jeremy had been to them.

He went to the back window and looked out. That was dumb because outside the window was the yard and the clothesline, not the street, but he felt that Mack might turn up pretty much anywhere.

"I just wish he'd hurry up," he said. "It's boring waiting." He opened his school lunch and ate it. The apple had bruises in it, and he cut them all out so carefully there was hardly any apple left.

Rosalie carried Oliver upstairs for his afternoon nap, and Jeremy took a walk around the block, keeping a watch out for vans. All the kids were still in school and the streets were quiet. He came back and tried to read, but he couldn't pay attention. The television was all soap operas, and he didn't know what was happening in them. Rosalie had her little black notebook out, but she wasn't writing anything.

The school bus went by, taking kids home. Even if he'd gone to school, he'd have been here in time for Mack. Oliver woke up and Rosalie put him in his stroller and pushed him down to Spring Street for some air. Jeremy went with them so he wouldn't be alone in the house. The sun was shining. Flowers were blooming in people's gardens. It looked as if nothing too awful could happen to anyone around here. Maybe Mack would just never show up, maybe it was all a joke.

When they got back, Rosalie started dinner.

"Maybe he won't be able to find the house," said Jeremy. "Maybe he doesn't know the address."

"Make sense," she said. "He's seen it plenty of times on letters. And you can't forget an address like 1000 Church Street. Put Oliver in his highchair, will you?"

"Already?"

"Yes. I don't want to be eating when . . ." Her voice wandered off and she didn't say it, and she laid forks and napkins on the table.

It was after six and they were clearing the table when Mack came.

Jeremy had been thinking he'd hear the van, because he'd been hearing it in his head for days, but he didn't.

They heard two hard knocks at the front door, and then it opened, and boots came *clonk*, *clonk* across the living room. Mack stood in the kitchen doorway and put his hands on the sides of it.

He really did look like a cowboy in a movie, or the hero on a television soap opera. He had pale-colored eyes, the way Rosalie said, and dark hair, and even

Jeremy could see that girls would think he was good-looking. He was wearing a white shirt with silver patterns on it and snaps instead of buttons. The snaps were open so his chest showed.

Oliver didn't like strangers and started to cry. Rosalie took him out of his highchair and hugged him and stared over his head at Mack.

"Where's my kiss?" he said. "Aren't you going to give Mack a kiss, coming so far?"

Rosalie looked at Jeremy, but he couldn't help, so she moved slowly across the floor to Mack in the doorway, and leaned over Oliver and gave him a sort of a kiss. She looked like someone tasting a lemon.

"That's my girl," said Mack, smiling down at her. "I knew you'd be glad to see old Mack. But what's that you're wearing? That's no dress, that's jeans. I told sonny here to tell you to wear a pretty dress for Mack. What's the matter? You saving up your pretty dress to wear for someone else?"

"I forgot," said Jeremy. "I forgot to tell her."

Mack turned and looked down at him. "You forgot," he said. His voice was so soft and sad you could hardly hear it. "Mack asks you to do one simple little thing, and you forget."

"I'm sorry!"

"I guess you don't think Mack's important, right? It doesn't matter what he wants."

"No, I mean, I don't know. I just forgot."

"Next time I better help you remember, I guess," he whispered. "See, Rosie's a pretty girl, and I like her to wear a pretty dress, and she wants to do what I like because that's how girls are. So next time I tell you something to do, you'll remember. Right?"

"I guess," said Jeremy, because he had to say something. He smiled nervously.

"Something's funny? Something's funny about Mack?"

"No. Oh no."

"That's good. Mack doesn't like to be laughed at." He turned back to Rosalie. "So how's my boy Joe? He miss his daddy?"

"His name's Oliver," said Rosalie in a very little voice.

"You can call him Oliver if you want. Call him Petunia if you want. But his daddy calls him Joe, because if there's one thing I hate it's a sissy. I hate a sissy even worse than a liar." He turned his pale-colored eyes on Jeremy for a minute, and then reached for the baby.

Oliver's face crumpled up and he clung to Rosalie. Mack pulled at him, but she held on, saying, "Wait, he doesn't know you. He has to get used to people."

"I never heard of a kid that didn't know his own daddy." He got a grip around Oliver's middle and said, "You better let go so he doesn't get hurt."

He pulled Oliver away, and the baby screamed and doubled up his knees.

"Cut that out!" said Mack. "Make him stop that yell-
ing, I can't stand it. I'm real nervous. Jail does your
nerves that way." Oliver screamed harder. "Hey, this
is your daddy, Joe. Come to take you off to Texas. Give
me a kiss." Oliver stopped crying long enough to pull
back and stare at him, and then started thrashing and
twisting to get away.

"He'll fall, give him back to me," cried Rosalie.

"Here, take him," said Mack, disgusted. "Crybaby."
He sat down at the table and said, "What did you make
for my dinner?"

"We already ate," said Rosalie.

"Potatoes," said Jeremy quickly. "We've got lots of
potatoes left."

Mack laughed. "That's no dinner for a grown man.
She'll find something better than that, my Rosie. Girls
always like to feed a man."

Rosalie put Oliver back in his highchair and opened
the refrigerator and looked inside, and slowly took
some things out and put them on the counter. Jeremy
could see that her hands were shaking.

"Anybody'd think you wasn't expecting me," said
Mack. "After I spent all that money phoning." He took
a comb with a big curved handle out of his back pocket
and ran it through his hair, and then pushed the side
hair into shape with his hands. "Okay, sonny," he said
to Jeremy. "Just to show we're going to be buddies, I'll

64

teach you to arm-wrestle." He unsnapped the cuff of his shirt and rolled it up neatly and set his elbow on the table. "Ready?"

There wasn't much choice, so Jeremy put his elbow down too, and Mack took hold of his hand. His fingers were as hard as iron, and he crunched Jeremy's knuckles together. It was like getting your hand caught in a trap, or some kind of machinery. Mack pressed, and Jeremy tried to press back, but just for a minute, because it was no use, and then his arm banged down on the table.

Mack held it there, pushing the knuckles into the wood. His face was close up to Jeremy's now, and Jeremy could see how long and thin his mouth was, and turned up at the corners so he seemed to be smiling all the time, like an alligator.

"Let go," said Jeremy. "That hurts!"

"What hurts?" He was grinding harder, and Jeremy half-rose out of his chair. "That doesn't hurt. When Mack has to hurt somebody, he can hurt them all right, but this is just play. Just a game."

Rosalie came from the stove with a plate of bacon and eggs, and Mack let go and picked up his fork.

Jeremy could see the tears of pain in his own eyes. He blinked to keep them from falling, and rubbed his sore hand quietly under the table.

Eight

ROSALIE TOOK OLIVER upstairs to put him to bed.

Mack ate, and said with his mouth full, "Not too strong, are you, sonny? I guess we better take you along to Texas. Put you to work on the oil rigs and toughen you up."

"I have to go to school," said Jeremy.

"School," said Mack. "Huh. Look at me, I never set foot in school after seventh grade. Just drove by sometimes to pick up girls. School's okay for girls. It gives them something to do till they get married. Boys, it just makes them soft."

He pushed his plate away and propped one foot up on a chair and polished the boot with his napkin. His boots had big square heels on them like a kid's building blocks. He polished the other one and dropped the napkin on the table.

From upstairs they could hear Rosalie singing to Oliver.

Mack said, "She sure is taking her time. I guess I'll go on up, we got some talking to do. I still can't figure why she ran off like she did. And why you kept telling those lies when I called. But we're going to get it all straightened out." He pushed his chair back and went upstairs.

Alone, Jeremy sat and listened to their voices from Rosalie's room. He thought he heard her crying. He took Mack's egg-smeared plate to the sink and ran water over it. His knuckles were red and sore and starting to swell up.

He turned on the dishwasher, and the rushing and growling sounds drowned out the voices from upstairs. For the first time ever he wished he had some home-work to do. Something else to think about.

He tried to call Kevin to find out what the math assignment was but the phone was busy. Kevin's sister blabbing, probably. Kevin had a normal kind of sister who just had boyfriends, not a husband, and hung out at the shopping mall and talked on the phone a lot.

He dialed again, but it was still busy. He got out the King Arthur book and opened it in the middle of an adventure and tried to read, but he kept wondering what was happening upstairs. If Mack was hurting Rosalie, maybe there was something he should do about it.

Finally his mother came home.

She took her shoes off the way she always did and said, "Are you still up? There's a van parked outside. Did Mack get here?"

"He's upstairs," said Jeremy.

She went to the stairs and called up, "Rosalie? I want to meet your young man. Bring him down."

Rosalie had changed her clothes. She was wearing a pretty dress. Mack shook hands with Jeremy's mother and said, "Pleasure to meet you, ma'am." He smiled at her with his long alligator smile. He had beautiful white teeth.

Jeremy's mother smiled back as if she didn't want to but couldn't stop herself. "I understand you're planning to take Rosalie and the baby off to Texas."

"Yes, ma'am. Sorry it's so far away, but I figure I can get work there."

Jeremy's mother said, "Don't you think it would be wiser if you went first, and then sent for them after you get work?"

"Well, ma'am," said Mack, and looked down at his boots as if he were shy. "We've been apart a long time, me and her. Seems it would be nice if we could be together again. I sure did miss her."

"Of course," said Jeremy's mother. "I do understand that. I was just worrying about the baby."

"I'll take real good care of them, ma'am. You don't need to worry." He smiled and showed his white teeth again.

"Mom," said Rosalie. "Mother. Please. I don't want to go."

"But why not?"

"She feels strange with me, I guess," said Mack. "Away so long. You know how girls are."

"Of course, that's natural. But Rosalie, honey, I'm sure you'll love Texas. I've always wanted to see it myself."

Rosalie made a strange noise like a cat choking. "I think I hear Oliver," she said, and ran away back upstairs.

"Oh dear," said Jeremy's mother. "Well, I expect everything will work out for the best. Can I make you a cup of coffee?"

"Why, that would be swell, ma'am," said Mack. "But I don't want to put you to the trouble."

"Oh, it's no trouble, heavens," said Jeremy's mother, and turned away to put the kettle on the stove.

Mack ran his comb through his hair again and winked at Jeremy. He looked pleased with himself, as if he'd pulled off a smart trick.

Jeremy said, "I have to go to bed," and went upstairs.

Rosalie was in the bathroom. He saw the light under the door and knocked. "Rosalie?"

"Jerry? Come in. Close the door behind you." She was sitting on the laundry hamper.

"Mom likes him," he said, and sat down on the edge of the tub.

"I used to like him myself. He can do that to people, it's like a game he plays. Jeremy, I'm so scared."

"What are you going to do?"

"I don't know. I can't go clear to Texas with him, and nobody there to help. He said he was going to keep me locked up so I don't run away again, or go out with other men."

"He can't, it's against the law. Isn't it?"

"Not if the law doesn't know about it."

"You could call them."

"Not if there isn't any phone." She chewed her fingernails.

"There's the fort," said Jeremy slowly. "The fort Kelly and I made."

"What about it?"

"You could hide there for a while. Just till you thought of something else." It wasn't the greatest idea in the world, and he wasn't young enough to think you could live there, with no toilet or anything, but at least it was secret.

"Suppose he finds me?"

"He can't find you." Jeremy tried to sound sure of it, but he wasn't really. "Wait till he goes to sleep, and then get Oliver and come scratch on my door and I'll take you."

"What if he wakes up?"

"Then he catches us," said Jeremy. "You better go on downstairs now before he gets mad." Since when am I the boss? Jeremy wondered. But somebody had to be the boss, and Rosalie was too scared to think.

She nodded and splashed water on her face and went out.

Jeremy brushed his teeth and went to bed with his clothes on.

From downstairs he heard Mack's voice and his mother's. Probably she was asking about his trip, and he was saying, "Yes, ma'am," and "Thank you, ma'am," and being all sweet and shy. She'd be thinking what a nice-looking, polite young man he was, even if he had been in jail.

He didn't hear Rosalie's voice. She'd just be sitting there biting her nails.

He lay in bed with the covers up to his chin so no one could see he had his clothes on, and tried to think of what might happen. What would Mack do when he woke up in the morning and they were gone? Would he blame Jeremy? It would be safer if he stayed in the fort too.

It didn't help any to worry. If you thought about something too much before you did it, you got too worried to do anything.

Better just to think about getting them all to the fort. There was a flashlight in the kitchen on top of the refrigerator. It would be like sleeping out in the back-yard. Only when you slept in the backyard, you could always get up and go back inside if it was cold or you heard funny noises or wanted a drink of water.

Weren't they ever going to go to bed?

At last he heard Rosalie coming up the stairs. Brushing her teeth.

Then he heard Mack saying, "Good night, ma'am, and thank you for the coffee," and coming up.

His mother would be putting the coffee cups in the sink. Locking the doors, turning out the lights.

Finally she came up too. She didn't call in to say good night because she thought he was asleep by now. After a while the crack of light under his door went out. The house was dark and quiet.

He lay still, waiting. Listening for Rosalie. He heard whispers and sheets rustling. Then nothing. Except his own heart beating. He turned over on his side and heard his eyelashes scratching on the pillow. A car went by outside and its lights crossed his ceiling.

Suddenly he was falling asleep. His eyelids went thick and fat as pillows and pushed against his eyes.

It would be safer to sit up.

He sat on the edge of his bed in the dark with his face in his hands and watched the glowing second hand of his alarm clock jerking around and around the dial. It made a tiny, cross, buzzing sound in the quiet room.

Sometimes he fell asleep and pitched forward with a jerk, and woke up again. The clock hand moved slower and slower.

Nine

THE CLOCK SAID twenty minutes after two when Rosalie scratched lightly on Jeremy's door.

He felt his way across the room and opened it.

It was even darker in the hall, with no windows. He reached for Rosalie's arm and instead touched Oliver, who snuffled and whimpered, half asleep.

He and Rosalie felt their way along the wall for the stairs. They could hear their mother's breathing, and grunting snores from Mack. "Hurry," Jeremy whispered.

"I can't," Rosalie breathed back. "I'm afraid to fall with Oliver."

Some of the stairs creaked. Oliver whimpered again.

Downstairs it was brighter, from the streetlight outside. Jeremy crept across the room toward the kitchen, handing himself along from chair to couch to doorway, and felt on the top of the refrigerator for the flashlight. A package of napkins fell softly to the floor. There was the flashlight. Only something was wrong with it. It didn't feel heavy enough. He pressed the switch and nothing happened. No batteries. He'd borrowed the batteries for something else a long time ago and never put them back.

"We'll have to go in the dark," he whispered. "It's safer anyway. Someone might see the light."

"Matches. We can take some matches," Rosalie said. "They're in this drawer here."

"Okay, but we can't light one till we're in the fort."

They unlocked the kitchen door and crept outside, closing the screen gently behind them.

"It's cold," said Rosalie.

"I guess we should have brought blankets."

"We can't go back now."

They felt the path ahead of them with their feet and made their way out of the dark bushes and onto the sidewalk under the streetlight. If Mack looked out the window, he could see the three of them bright as day.

Jeremy wanted to run as fast as he could, but Rosalie wouldn't run with the baby. They hunched over and hurried out of the light into the safe dark, and then into the shine of the next streetlight.

"How far is it?"

"Down at Spring Street. Maple and Spring. You know, the vacant lot."

Most of the houses were dark. Here and there someone had left a light on, in a bathroom or a hall, but the people would be asleep. If he and Rosalie yelled for help, no one would hear them. It was the middle of the night. Jeremy said it to himself, "the middle of the night," and it made his hair prickle. They were wearing sneakers, so they didn't even have their own footsteps to listen to. They walked as silently as if they were invisible, and passed through the middle of the night without leaving a mark on it.

At the end of the block Jeremy looked over his shoulder. His own house was still dark. Mack was still asleep. He wouldn't stay asleep forever, though.

The streetlight at the corner of Maple showed nothing but the patch of dark woods. No one would see them in there, at least not by night. Maybe not by day either. But how long could they stay?

"Isn't there a path?" asked Rosalie.

"Of course not. For people to see?"

"How do you get in, then?"

"It's along here somewhere. I'm not sure. Ow!" He had walked into a blackberry bush.

"Be quiet," said Rosalie.

"Why?"

"I thought I heard footsteps."

They listened, but there was nothing.

"Come on, we just have to push our way in," said Jeremy. "Watch out for poison ivy."

"How am I supposed to do that? And what about Oliver? He'll get scratched."

"Put your shirt over his face."

She did, and Oliver complained with muffled sounds.

"Hold on to my sweater and follow me," said Jeremy, and pushed into the woods with his arm over his eyes against prickers.

It was only a tiny woods, a leftover place people had forgotten to build houses on, but when you couldn't see anything it felt like the whole Amazon jungle. Twice Jeremy almost fell down and pulled Rosalie with him. She was stretching his sweater out of shape, hanging on. Then he accidentally let a branch whip back and slap her in the face. Prickers pulled at his sleeves. He kept pushing forward, or maybe around in circles, with one arm out in front of him feeling for the fort.

When he finally walked into it, he almost broke his wrist.

Even then it took forever to find the bush that hid the entrance, and to crawl through it onto the cold cement floor.

Inside, he struck a match.

Rosalie looked a mess. Her hair was all pulled into fuzz from prickers, and there were scratches on her face and a red stripe across her forehead from where the branch slapped her.

She looked at him and said, "Your face is all scratched."

"Yours too. Watch out for Glatisant."

"Who? Oh, your snake. I didn't know he was so big. You ought to get a bigger tank."

Jeremy's blue jacket that he never took home was in Glatisant's corner. Just before the match burned his fingers, Jeremy grabbed it and put it on in the dark.

"This is silly," said Rosalie. "I feel like a little kid, hiding out in a hut in the woods. Playing armies."

"It's not a hut, it's a fort. You got any better ideas?"

"I was thinking, if I could get to Missy's house —"

"Your freaky friend? She lives in Eastbourne, doesn't she?"

"If someone would drive me. If Mom would drive me."

"Why would she? She thinks Mack's just great."

Oliver fussed, and Rosalie jiggled him and sang,

Sleepy as morning stars,
Quiet as dew,
Grass flowers folded up
Pinky and blue,
Deep in the grass in the
Nighttime like you.
Fly away, Oliver,
Sleepy old Oliver,

Gone where the butterflies,
Butterflies flew.

There were smacking sounds; Oliver had found his thumb and was sucking it.

Rosalie said, "If *you* talked to Mom. If you told her Mack's crazy and I can't go with him, she'd listen to you, maybe. She thinks I'm silly, but you're a boy. Sensible."

"Terrific. And where's Mack while I'm talking to Mom? Just standing there smiling?"

"He'll sleep late. He's been sleeping in the van, he's tired. You just get there early and wait till she comes downstairs, and tell her. Tell her if she drives me to Missy's I can stay awhile, and he won't be able to find me."

"And then he comes downstairs and cuts me up into cat food with a chain saw. And Mom too. Swell."

"But Jerry, what else can we do? I can't stay here forever!"

"You go tell her yourself, then." What was he doing here? He was cold and he was scared and a crazy man was waiting to hurt him, so he couldn't go back to the house, and it was all Rosalie's fault. "You're older than I am," he said. "And you're supposed to be this genius or something, so you go off and marry a crazy person and have a baby, and then you want *me* to do something about it? I'm only a kid." He stood up and bumped his head on the low side of the roof.

"But somebody has to help me."

He couldn't see her, but it sounded as if she was crying. He didn't care. "Get somebody else, then."

"There isn't anybody else. Mom won't listen to me, she thinks I'm too whifty to know what I want. And she hates to think about anything awful or scary. Like when Dad was getting ready to leave, she just wouldn't notice. She pretends everything's okay all the time." She was really crying now. "And I have to go back to school. I have to finish college if I'm going to be a writer. I can't go to school if I'm locked up in a van in Texas."

"You can't go anyway. You can't take a baby to college."

"I can so. I can get another scholarship, and take Oliver, and find girls to stay with him while I'm in class."

"No you can't, because Mack won't let you. Listen, I'm getting out of here. I'm going over to Kevin's and sleep there, and stay there till Mack goes away."

He wanted to get out of this. Just away, anywhere. Get clear away from Mack and Rosalie and everyone, and not have anything to do with them until it was safe again.

Kevin's was a long walk, though. And if he rang the bell at four o'clock in the morning they wouldn't exactly be glad to see him. They'd call his mother to come get him. She might even send Mack to get him.

Rosalie sniffled in the dark. "Please, Jeremy. She'll listen to you. She thinks boys have more sense than girls. Thinks they can fix the toaster and stuff like that."

"I can't."

"I know. But she doesn't. Please."

How did he get mixed up in this anyway? What was the first thing he did wrong? Answering the phone, maybe. That first time he said Rosalie was out when she wasn't. He shouldn't even have talked to Mack. Just stayed out of it. And now look.

She was his sister, of course. She used to take him to the zoo. When she went away to college, she'd given him her whole collection of Peanuts books and the tiger poster, and the chameleons that died, and a lot of tapes and records he never played. There was also the time he cut his hand sharpening a pencil with the carving knife, and she'd stopped the bleeding by squeezing it hard and putting ice on it, and got blood all over her sweater.

He sighed. "Okay. I'll go. I'll try to get her to come."

Maybe she would. Maybe it would all be okay. Mom would take Rosalie away out of reach, and then tell Mack to get out, and protect Jeremy. It would feel good to have somebody else in charge for a change.

"You'd better wait awhile," said Rosalie. "It's too early."

It was dark in the fort, but it was always dark in there. Outside it was beginning to be daylight. The doorway showed pale in the wall. But it was May, and the sun came up around four in the morning. They waited. Rosalie sang some more songs to Oliver. Glatisant moved in the leaves in his tank, making rustling sounds from the dark corner. Light from the door showed where he'd written in the cement, "Sir Jeremy the Black Knight of the Lake was here." Some knight, he thought. Hiding out scared.

He felt as if he'd been hiding scared for at least a hundred years.

Ten

GOING BACK, there was bright sunlight in the streets, but it was still very early, with no traffic. Robins were hopping around people's lawns looking for worms. Could Mack possibly still be asleep, with all this sunshine coming through his window? Or would he be up already? Storming around shouting for Rosalie? Waiting to get his hands on Jeremy?

Jeremy walked more and more slowly, scuffing his sneakers. It would be nice just never to get there. It would be nice just to suddenly wake up and be in his bed, and find out that it wasn't today at all but about two weeks ago, and have everything happen differently. Have Mack stay in Wyoming.

But it wasn't two weeks ago, it was now, and he

couldn't push it backward. All he could do was hope that Mack was still asleep and his mother was up and in the kitchen. Then he would just explain to her that Rosalie wasn't being silly about Mack, and she'd understand. She'd put her coat on and go rescue Rosalie and take her to Missy's.

Only, what would they do about Mack afterward?

He'd better not think about that.

He turned down Church Street, slowly, and there was his house in the sunshine, with a robin on the lawn. And Mack's van parked in front. He walked past it, and around the bushes to the other side.

The driveway was empty. His mother's car was gone.

Of course. It was Tuesday. Tuesday and Thursday she had to be at work by seven, to say good morning to the patients when they came downstairs, and tell them what to do all day.

He stood still. Now there was no one at all to help. There ought to be someone, but his father lived in Baltimore since the divorce and his mother worked long hours. There was no one to take care of things but Jeremy, and he was only a kid. It wasn't fair.

It wasn't fair, but there it was. He had to do something.

If Rosalie was going to get to Missy's house, she'd have to wait till evening when their mother got home.

But if she was going to hide in the fort all day with Oliver, they'd need stuff to eat and drink. If he could sneak inside and get them some food, they could all hide out there and wait.

Then, at night, he could watch for his mother's car coming down Spring Street and stop her before she went home.

And what would Mack do all day? Never mind, he couldn't worry about everything. The first thing was to get some food. He stepped quietly along the path through the bushes to the kitchen door.

The door groaned a little on its hinges as he eased himself inside. The kitchen looked just as usual. The sun came in through the window, and his mother had left half a cup of coffee on the table.

He could carry more things if he used a bag, but opening a bag made too much noise. He'd have to take just what he could carry in his hands.

Bread. There was bread on the counter, easy to find. And some apples in a bowl on the table. The carton of milk in the refrigerator. Moving softly, he crossed the floor and eased open the refrigerator.

The flashlight fell down.

He must have left it sticking over the top of the door. It bounced, clattering, off the refrigerator shelves and crashed to the floor and echoed through the quiet house like gunshot.

Jeremy froze. Feet thumped on the stairs. Mack. He was coming down.

Jeremy shut the refrigerator door and pressed himself against it. There was the door, and he ought to run for it, but he couldn't. His knees were shaking so hard he might fall down. There was no place to hide, and no time.

The feet crossed the living room. Jeremy held his breath.

"Who's there? What happened?" And Mack stood in the doorway, his boots in his hand.

"Me," said Jeremy in a squeaking voice. His heart was beating so he shook all up and down. "I was just getting some breakfast. Can I get you some breakfast?"

Mack stared down at him, breathing hard through his nose. The whites glittered around his eyes like the eyes of a crazy horse. He wasn't so tall without his boots, but his shirt was open and the muscles on his chest bulged. "Where's Rosie?" he said.

"I don't know." Jeremy could hardly hear his own words.

"She's gone. She's not in the room. The kid's gone too."

"I don't know. I was just getting some —"

"Yeah," said Mack. He dropped his boots and pressed Jeremy up against the refrigerator with his strong hands. "You don't want to tell any more lies because the time for telling lies to Mack is over."

"Honest, I don't – "

"Mack hates to hurt people. You just say where Rosie's gone and then we'll be buddies again. But you better say it pretty soon because sometimes Mack gets mad and that's when people get hurt."

Very softly and gently he took hold of Jeremy's arm and bent it up behind his back. Leaning over, he whispered, "I bet you don't like to get hurt, because you're kind of a sissy. Sissies don't like to get hurt." He pushed Jeremy's arm upward. "Where's Rosie?"

Jeremy squeezed his eyes shut and didn't answer.

"Mack hates to do this, because Mack is a real nice guy when people treat him right. But you don't treat me right, sonny. Do you?" He pushed harder. Jeremy crouched down and twisted around trying to stop the pain. "Do you?" Mack gave a quick little jerk upward, to show how much more it could hurt than it already did.

Jeremy tried to think about King Arthur and Sir Launcelot, and how they would never tell. But they weren't kids. They were grown-up men in armor with swords. Nobody bent their arm up behind them. It was easy to be brave if you could fight back.

In his soft voice Mack said, "I could push just a tiny bit more – like this – "

"Don't! Please! It hurts!"

"And then your arm would likely come clean out

of your shoulder and fall on the floor. Now where's Rosie?"

"In the fort," gasped Jeremy.

Mack let go and smiled his long alligator smile. "Doesn't take much to make you tell, does it? That's good. I was afraid I might have to hurt you some."

Jeremy was panting. He leaned against the refrigerator and rubbed his shoulder.

When he had thought about Mack coming, he'd thought he might have a gun. But he didn't even need a gun. He got everything he wanted just with his hands. It was the same old stuff every bully on the playground knew about. Only Mack was stronger, and there weren't any teachers here to make him stop before he broke your arm.

Mack took a key out of his pants pocket and slapped it down on the table. "Now we're going to take a little ride. Soon as I get my boots on." He sat down and pulled on one boot. "You're going to show me where this fort is, because I know my little wife wants to see her husband. And if she doesn't, then she ought to."

There was a knock on the door, and then Kelly pushed it open and came in. For a second Jeremy was happy to see her, but what could Kelly do? She might make things worse. Make Mack madder. "What do you want?" he said rudely.

"Some meat. Hullo," she added to Mack. "Jeremy,

have you got any meat? I have to go to you-know-where and get Mom's bucket before school, and Glassident doesn't have anything to eat. Is there any hamburger or anything?"

"What's this you-know-where business?" asked Mack.

Kelly looked uncomfortable. "It's a secret," she said.

"Yeah? And maybe this secret's got something to do with where my wife's gone?"

"Your wife? You mean Rosalie? Jeremy, did you take Rosalie to the —" She stopped herself.

Jeremy couldn't think what to say, so he didn't say anything.

Mack lurched over to Kelly on his one boot and one bare foot and put his hand under her chin. "You don't want to have secrets from Mack, do you? Pretty little girl like you. Pretty girls never have secrets from a nice-looking fellow like Mack. Now where's this you-know-where place you were headed for?"

Kelly backed away from his hand. "I can't tell you."

Jeremy looked at the key to the van, lying on the table beside his mother's coffee cup.

If he could drive the van, he could rescue Rosalie.

He could drive it over to the woods and grab Rosalie and Oliver and take them to Missy's house in East-bourne. Mack would never find them.

It was against the law. He was way too young to drive, and besides, it was stealing. But maybe he could explain to the police and they wouldn't mind.

Mack said to Kelly, "Now Jeremy's going to show me this place his own self, pretty soon. But maybe you'll tell me about it first, so he doesn't try any more tricks."

"I *said*, it's a *secret*," said Kelly.

Jeremy grabbed the key and raced out the door.

Eleven

THE VAN WAS right out front. Jeremy scrambled in behind the wheel and poked the key into the ignition. He turned it and pumped the gas pedal. It started, and he was surprised; he hadn't really expected it to start.

From inside the house he heard a crash that sounded like a chair falling over, and a yell that sounded like Kelly.

He pushed the clutch in, shoved the gearshift up, and let the clutch out. The van jumped in the air and died. Wrong gear.

The back door banged and Kelly came pelting down the path with her hair flying.

He started the engine again.

The door banged a second time and Mack came out,

hopping and hobbling on one boot, carrying the other and shouting.

Kelly grabbed the passenger's door of the van and stuck her head in. "What are you doing?" she cried.

This time he found the right gear and the van bucked slowly down Church Street. Kelly clung to the door.

Jeremy turned the van down Oakland Street, still in first gear because he was afraid to shift. As he turned he caught a glimpse of Mack behind him. He was bent over pulling on his other boot.

Kelly dragged herself head first in through the window and landed on the seat in a heap. "You can't drive," she said.

"I can so," said Jeremy, without taking his eyes off the street ahead. He had to sit way forward to see out at all. He held the steering wheel tightly in both hands, but even so the van kept wobbling back and forth. It was lucky there wasn't any traffic.

Kelly leaned out the window to look back. "He's after us," she said. "He just came round the corner. He sees us. Here he comes!"

Jeremy turned the wrong direction, left down Green Street, and went a little faster. Taking a chance, he shifted gears, and by luck he found second. The van smoothed out some and stopped roaring.

"Who says I can't drive?" he said. He turned right onto Maple. "Is he still coming?"

Kelly looked back. "I don't see him."

He was driving. He sat up high above the street, and the van did what he told it to do, though his steering still wavered from side to side.

When he was older and had a license he could go wherever he wanted to go. Faster than a knight on horseback, he could travel all over the country. He could go to the places Mack had gone across. The states with names that sounded like Indians and the wind. Dakota, Wyoming, Colorado. They weren't just drawings on a map, but solid ground like his own front lawn. A person in a car could drive to them, and get out and stand on them. Climb up the mountains. Wash his face in the rivers.

"Slow down," said Kelly. She was holding on to the dashboard.

At the corner of Maple and Spring he wobbled into the weeds at the side of the street, and the van shuddered and gave a kick and stopped. He'd forgotten to push the clutch down. He jumped out and plunged into the woods, with Kelly behind him.

"He'll see the van," she said. "We ought to hide it."

"No time." Stumbling through the blackberries, with their curved thorns like fishhooks that clawed at his clothes, Jeremy pushed his way to the fort and crawled in through the doorway. "Come on," he said. "Rosalie, come quick! I've got the van!"

Rosalie stopped changing Oliver's diaper and stared at him. "The van? Mack's van? But where's Mother?"

"She wasn't home, it's Tuesday. Come on, I don't have time to explain. I'm going to take you to Missy's in the van!"

"But you can't drive."

"I did, didn't I?"

"If we're going anywhere, I'm driving," Rosalie said. "But how did you get it? Where's Mack?"

"Looking for us. Hurry up!"

"Wait a second." She finished putting Oliver's dry diaper on and then shook out his red woolly sleeping bag and started to poke his legs into it.

"Do you have to do that?" asked Jeremy. "Just bring him the way he is."

"He'd freeze." Oliver kicked his fat legs out of the sleeping bag, and she pushed it back on again. She pulled it up over his stomach and fumbled with the zipper in the half-dark of the fort.

"Hurry."

"I'm hurrying. The zipper's stuck."

"Rosalie!"

"Okay, wait, I have to get my jacket."

"Never mind your jacket!"

"My notebook's in it."

Kelly pushed herself in through the doorway. "Move over," she whispered. "He's here."

"Where?"

"Be quiet. He came running down Spring Street and saw the van. Now he's coming into the woods."

They sat still, hunched together in the fort. They could hear Mack crashing in the woods and swearing horribly at the prickers. "I see you!" he called. "You better come out of there, sonny, if you want to stay in one piece. You too, Rosie. I know you're there."

"He doesn't see us," Kelly breathed in Jeremy's ear. "He's lying."

The fort sat in the darkest, prickliest part of the little woods, with blackberries growing all over its walls and across its roof. It looked like another, thicker clump of brambles.

"I don't want to have to come get you," said Mack's voice. It sounded farther away this time. "Because that way I might get mad. So you'd better come out by the time I count three. One."

Jeremy, Kelly, and Rosalie tried to breathe quietly.

"Two." They heard him stumble like a bear and curse again. Probably he'd stepped in the swampy part by the big stump.

"Three! Okay, I'm coming." But he didn't sound close.

Maybe he'd give up. Get tired of looking, and get in the van and go away.

It was cramped in the fort, and Jeremy's shoulder

hurt where Mack had twisted it. He moved, trying to get comfortable, and his elbow hit Oliver.

Oliver started to cry.

His shrieks rang out like a siren. Rosalie squeezed him against her shoulder and tried to hush him, but he kept crying. For a second he stopped to suck in his breath, and they could hear Mack outside the fort, laughing.

Then the bushes moved by the doorway. They were trapped.

Mack's head and shoulders blocked the light, and his arm reached in and grabbed Kelly, who was closest.

She dropped her head onto his hand and he yelled out. She had bitten him. He didn't let go, though; his strong hands clutched her by the arm and coat and dragged her outside. Jeremy could hear her fall into the bushes, and then go crashing away running.

Mack crawled inside where Kelly had been. Even in the half-darkness his eyes were shining pale and wild-looking. His hand was bleeding.

"Get up," he said to Rosalie. "We're leaving."

"But Mack —"

"You're lucky I'm taking you away from these freaks. Come on, move. We're going to Texas. I've stood enough."

Rosalie shrank back up against the wall. Her voice was shaky but she said, "I don't want to. I want to go back to college."

"Leave her alone," said Jeremy, but he didn't say it very loud and Mack didn't notice.

"Girls don't know what they want. That's why they need a husband to tell them what to do. Now are you coming?"

"No," she whispered.

Mack crouched down close to her and said in his soft voice, "I think you're going to change your mind. I think you're going to want to come along. Because . . ."

And in a flash he had snatched Oliver out of her lap and held him up high. "Because this kid's going to Texas with his daddy!"

Twelve

Rosalie sat stiff, staring as if she didn't understand.

Oliver cried and struggled, and Mack clamped him under his arm and backed toward the doorway, bent over. "Quiet down, kid," he said. "We got a long trip ahead, you and me."

"Hey," said Jeremy. "You can't do that. You can't take Oliver."

"You going to stop me, sonny?" To Rosalie, he said, "This is the last chance you get. You can come along with your husband where you belong. Or you don't see the kid anymore."

Rosalie didn't seem to be able to move or say anything.

Suddenly Jeremy was mad. He was so mad he could hardly breathe. He was mad all over again at the fifth-grade bullies who had picked on him when he was little and couldn't stop them. He was mad at them and at Mack, and at everyone who was mean and nobody could stop them because they were stronger.

He groped wildly around the dark walls for a weapon, and his hand hit the bucket. Kelly's mother's bucket. It was a dumb thing to use, but it was all there was.

He grabbed it and jumped straight at Mack and banged it down over his head.

Mack was crouched over already, and off balance. He staggered blindly and reached for the wall, and Oliver wiggled out from under his arm like a fish.

Rosalie threw herself forward and snatched Oliver out of the air, and scrunched back into the corner holding the baby tight.

Mack's thrashing arm missed the wall and he toppled over. His shoulder hit Glatisant's tank. Broken glass spattered onto the cement.

Mack pulled the bucket off his head, and his pale eyes in the dark found Jeremy. "All right, sonny," he said. "You asked for it. Now Mack is going to plain take you apart."

He moved to get up, but then he gave a horrible shrill scream like an animal and fell back.

He was lying there with his head and shoulders in

the broken glass, and Glatisant was pouring smoothly past his face with his tongue flickering. He flickered at Mack's ear, testing it to see what it was.

"Snake!" Mack screamed. "Snake! Get it, get it away!"

Jeremy reached over and grabbed Glatisant close behind his head so he couldn't bite, and the snake wrapped itself around his arm.

"Get it out of here!" cried Mack. "I can't stand snakes. Get it out!"

It was then that Rosalie started to laugh. For a second Jeremy was afraid she was having some kind of fit. It seemed like a strange time to laugh. But that was what she was doing, just laughing so hard she couldn't sit up straight. She rocked back and forth, holding Oliver, and kept on laughing helplessly.

"Shut that up," said Mack, and scrambled to his feet with bits of glass falling off him. "Shut up, I said!"

"I can't, I can't help it," she gasped. "You should have seen yourself. Just a garter snake, a poor little garter snake. Oh, I can't stop!"

"Nobody laughs at Mack!"

"But you looked so silly."

Mack crouched over and slapped her so hard her head snapped sideways. She couldn't stop laughing, but there were tears in her eyes.

"I'll fix you so you never laugh again!"

Glatisant was still squirming, trying to get away.

Jeremy shouted, "No, you won't, either!" and threw his arm up and flung the snake at Mack. It struck him full in the face and dropped down twisting over his shoulder.

Mack sprang back with his eyes wild and threw his shoulder into the wall. There was a great ripping, cracking sound and the wall, Kelly's wall, gave way and fell down with a crash. The roof crackled and sagged. Glatisant dropped to the floor.

In the sudden bright light Mack's face looked white and weird. Sweat stood out all over it in shiny globs. He scrambled over the fallen boards and plunged into the woods.

Rosalie was wiping her eyes on her shoulders. Safe in her lap, Oliver sucked his thumb.

"You okay?" asked Jeremy. "There's blood on your face."

She wiped it off and looked at her fingers. "I think it's Mack's. From where Kelly bit him. Oh, poor Mack, didn't he look *silly*?"

"You're lucky he didn't knock your head off."

"*My* head? Who hit him with a bucket? Who threw a snake in his face?"

"I guess you're right." The full force of what he'd done came over him, and he had to sit down. "Well, anyway," he said weakly, "you're the one that laughed."

"I had you and Glatisant with me. Oh, Jeremy, King Arthur would be proud of you!"

From over by the street they heard the van start up and roar away. Its tires squealed at the corner.

Glatisant tested the boards of the fallen wall, looking for a way out.

"The tank's broken," said Jeremy. "There's no place to keep him."

"Let him go. It can be his reward."

"What if we need him again? What if Mack comes back?"

"He won't. We embarrassed him. And if he does, we'll get another snake. Or maybe just a caterpillar would do." Rosalie giggled and clutched her side. "Ouch, don't let me start laughing. You know, Jerry, I don't think I'll ever be scared of anyone again."

"I know what you mean," said Jeremy. He set Glatisant in the doorway and watched him slip away like water over the leafy ground and into the bushes.

It was hard to believe they'd won, they'd actually won. Jeremy kept rolling that idea around in his mind to see if it was true, and it was. It was a wonderful feeling, winning. He felt like a giant.

He heard footsteps, and bushes rustling, and then he saw Kelly pushing through the woods with a man close behind her. The man was wearing a bathrobe and there was shaving lather on half his face.

"I brought help," she called. "Where's Mack? Oh, my wall! What happened?"

"Mack's gone," said Jeremy. "He went out through the wall."

"What a mess," Kelly said. "Why couldn't he use the doorway? This is Mr. Welsh. He said he'd help. He lives down there. I couldn't find anybody else."

Mr. Welsh unhooked some blackberry thorns from his bathrobe and looked at the broken fort, and at Jeremy and Rosalie and the baby. "You seem to have settled things without me," he said.

Mr. Welsh was kind of old, and he didn't seem very strong. Maybe it was good he hadn't come earlier; he could have gotten hurt. Actually, Jeremy figured it was pretty brave of him to come at all.

"So you don't need help anymore?" Mr. Welsh asked.

Rosalie stood up, holding Oliver. "No, thank you," she said. "But thanks very much for coming."

"You're welcome," he said. "The young lady here seemed to think you had a problem. But if you don't –" He touched the lather on his face. "Perhaps I'll just go home and finish shaving."

"I'm sorry I bothered you," said Kelly.

"No bother," said Mr. Welsh. "In fact, I was rather pleased. It's been years since anyone thought I could help them. At my age, most people think I'm the one who needs help. Never mind, I can find my way out. If you need anything in the future, don't hesitate to call." Mr. Welsh tied his bathrobe sash closer and went away, ducking to dodge the low branches.

"What a nice man," said Rosalie.

Kelly kicked at the fallen boards. "This is going to be a pain to fix," she said. "Worse than building it to begin with, because we have to be careful of the other walls. And the roof." She shook its overhanging edge and it creaked and shifted. "We might have to start clear over with the roof."

Jeremy groaned, and then yawned. "I'm sleepy," he said.

"I'm hungry," said Rosalie. "In fact, I'm starved. So's Oliver. Let's go make some breakfast."

"I want to hear what happened," said Kelly. "I missed all the fun."

Thirteen

THE DAY HAD properly started as they walked home, with people waving from doorways and other people starting their cars and driving to work. Some of them stared at Jeremy, Kelly, and Rosalie carrying the baby. They looked pretty strange, all scratched and draggled. There was still some blood on Rosalie's cheek, which was red from getting slapped. Jeremy's sneakers were untied and he kept stepping on the laces, but he was too tired to tie them.

He told Kelly how everything had happened, with Rosalie interrupting. When he told about hitting Mack with the bucket, Kelly stopped walking.

"I forgot the bucket. Mom sent me for the bucket so she could mop the kitchen floor. That's how I got mixed up in all this."

"You want to go back?" asked Jeremy. He didn't offer to go with her. He didn't want to see the fort again right now.

"No, I guess not. I'll get yelled at, but it doesn't matter. Mom washes that floor so much anyway she's going to make a hole through to the basement. So go on. What did Mack do then?"

They finished telling the story, and Kelly said, "Poor Glassident. I wonder if we'll see him again."

"Not if he has any sense, you won't," said Rosalie.

"Weren't you scared, Jeremy?" asked Kelly.

"I guess so," he said. "I don't know. Maybe I was too mad to be scared."

"Well, I was scared. When he dragged me out of the hut, I thought he was going to kill me. I bit him pretty hard. Blargh!" Kelly made faces with her mouth. "I hope he isn't poison. I better brush my teeth."

"You were both marvelous," said Rosalie.

They were home. "Are you coming in?" Rosalie asked Kelly. "I could make you some breakfast. Take the taste out of your mouth," she added, and giggled.

"No, I'd better get back. Mom'll have a fit. See you." And she went on down the sidewalk.

In the kitchen, Rosalie put Oliver in his highchair, just like on an ordinary day.

Their mother's coffee cup still sat on the table. Jeremy looked at it and thought it was sad and kind of lonesome that she didn't know. All those things had happened, and there she was at work thinking everything was the same as usual. He wondered if Sir Launcelot's mother ever knew what he was doing.

Just the same, it was nice to know that he could pretty much take care of things, even with Mom away so much.

"There's some bacon," said Rosalie. "And I'll make some toast, but Mack ate all the eggs."

Jeremy sat down at the table and started to play creepy-mouse with Oliver and then changed his mind.

"You really were a hero, Jerry," said Rosalie. "I just hope I never need to be rescued again."

"Maybe I'll rescue other people, then. For a job. Instead of just going to an office."

"I don't think there's any such job anymore," Rosalie said, and pushed down the toaster.

"Maybe there ought to be. After all, lots of people need rescuing." Sir Jeremy, he thought. Sir Jeremy the Black Knight of the Lake. Only he'd have a van instead of a horse, and drive all over the country.

"Da da da!" shouted Oliver, and tried to bang on the table with a soggy cracker.

Jeremy scratched his wrist. "I guess I better change my shirt for school," he said.

"Oh dear," said Rosalie. "I forgot. It's almost nine, you've missed the bus."

Again. It seemed like years since he'd been in school. He could hardly remember Kevin, or the teachers, so much had happened since. He scratched his wrist harder and looked down at it. Through the film of dirt he could see the little clear colorless bubbles forming. Poison ivy.

Rosalie put bacon and toast in front of him and sat down to eat and spoon cereal into Oliver's mouth. "Won't it be nice when the phone rings," she said, "and we know it's not Mack?"

Jeremy nodded with his mouth full. He was almost too tired to eat. He left his toast crusts on the plate and felt a tremendous yawn working its way up through his chest. When it got to his mouth, he yawned so hard he thought his jaws would come unfastened.

"I have to go to bed," he said.

"Da da!" cried Oliver, and blew cereal out onto his chin.

Jeremy climbed the stairs one at a time like an old man, and went to bed with his clothes on for the second time. These clothes must be as tired as I am, he thought.

He pulled the blanket over his face to shut out the sun and closed his eyes.

Deep down inside his head he could hear the rumble and rattle of the van again, only this time it was getting farther and farther away instead of closer. Just as he was falling asleep he saw that it wasn't Mack driving it now.

This time he, Jeremy, was driving, sitting up high behind the wheel. Rattling toward South Dakota, Colorado, Wyoming, Montana. Maybe even as far as Alaska. They were all waiting for him, out there across the mountains. And as soon as he was ready, he would go.